THE MOONLIT LABYRINTH

TZANGEL
The Moonlit Labyrinth

Written in the United States of America.

For more information or to book an event, contact:
Tzangel@gmail.com

Published by Spines
ISBN: 979-8-89569-089-5

The Moonlit Labyrinth

Revealing the Darkness

TZANGEL

CONTENTS

Dedication

*To those who weave the threads of love into the tapestry of magick
and to those who journey through shadowed labyrinths to reclaim their
inner light.
May your spirit be guided by the whispers of ancient stars
and the unwavering devotion of those who hold your heart dear.
This enchanted journey is for you.*

Acknowledgment

With every star that twinkles in the vastness above, I am reminded that each of us is born from the cosmic dance, star seeds planted with infinite potential and radiant magick. This journey has been a calling, a beckoning from the stars themselves to share the truth of our shared heritage—that we are all luminous, beautiful souls just waiting to awaken and remember.

To the Goddess, I bow in deep gratitude for my own awakening, for guiding me toward this path where I can share these magickal journeys with my cherished readers. Your light has illuminated every step of my way, and I feel your divine grace on every page.

To my beloved mother, whose spirit watches over me from realms unseen, thank you for the love and wisdom that shaped me. May your soul find peace among the stars, your laughter forever echoing in my heart.

To my family and friends, who have stood by me with unwavering love, you are the constellation that has guided me through the darkest nights. Your support has been a beacon, leading me back to myself every time I faltered.

To my readers, your loyalty and belief in these stories remind me daily that magick is alive and well in the world. May these pages awaken your own inner starlight and help you remember the beauty and power within.

Thank you, all of you, for sharing this journey with me. Let us continue to reach for the stars together.

Tzangel

Preface

In the mystical woods of Salem, Massachusetts, beneath ancient oaks in an enchanted grove, Soraya Avalon, High Priestess of the Coven of Solaria, orchestrates a ritual imbued with magick and tradition. But Soraya is no ordinary witch. She is the latest in a long, unbroken line of star seeds, beings whose spirits have journeyed across the cosmos for millennia, their essence forged in the distant light of the Milky Way Galaxy and the Orion Constellation. Her lineage has been woven through the fabric of human history, from the ancient temples of Atlantis to the shadowed trials of Salem, where her ancestors were persecuted for the very powers that now flow through her veins.

Tonight, as she calls upon the elemental forces that bind her coven in unity, she unknowingly taps into the vast reservoir of cosmic energy inherited from her ancestors. This energy, however, is a double-edged sword. Unbeknownst to Soraya, tonight's ritual will not just connect her to the Earth and her coven—it will also resonate across the dimensions, opening the gates to the Moonlit Labyrinth. In this shadowy domain, deception lurks like a serpent, waiting to strike.

This descent into darkness is no accident but a deliberate act of betrayal by Marina, a fellow coven member consumed by envy. Craving the ancient power that courses through Soraya's star seed blood, Marina allies herself with obscure forces, secretly infusing the ritual incense with a cursed substance. As the incense burns, releasing its fragrant plume into the night, Soraya's spirit is ensnared, violently pulled into the labyrinth, leaving her physical form collapsed amidst the fallen leaves.

The grove fills with the sounds of despair as her coven discovers her unmoving body. Gideon Thatcher, Soraya's staunch ally and covert admirer, grasps her hand, his whispered declarations of love mingling with vows to restore her. Little do they know that the key to saving Soraya lies not only in their loyalty but in the cosmic legacy she carries—a legacy that holds the secrets to transcending the labyrinth's twisted paths.

With Gideon's steadfast belief and the coven's unity, Soraya embarks on a perilous journey through the labyrinth. Guided by Zephyr, a mystical entity drawn from the mists, she confronts the betrayal that cast her into this spectral maze. As she navigates shifting paths and enigmatic challenges, Soraya unravels the complex web of her ancestry intertwined with Marina's dark vendetta, a feud that spans across eons and galaxies.

Empowered by the ancient knowledge of her star seed lineage, Soraya confronts the Abyssal Chasm, where malevolent shadows clutch at her spirit, and climbs the Celestial Tower to seek lost arcane knowledge that could counteract the curse. The Wyrd Woods test her resolve, demanding she severs the sinister magick Marina has woven into their sacred spaces.

With the Astral Sphere in hand, an artifact passed down through generations of star seeds, she harnesses the power of the Celestial Circle, casting a radiant light that purges the darkness. As you delve into these pages, step into a realm where magick dances with shadows, deceit shapes destinies, and love endures beyond the veils between worlds. Join Soraya and her coven as they confront the darkness, unravel twisted fates, and reclaim their legacy under the watchful gaze of the moonlit sky.

PROLOGUE

In the mystical woods of Salem, Massachusetts, where ancient oaks cast long shadows under the moonlit sky, Soraya Avalon, High Priestess of the Coven of Solaria, meticulously prepares her forest altar for a full moon ritual that will unknowingly alter her destiny. The coven, whose origins trace back to the Orion constellation, carries within it the ancient wisdom and magick of the stars. The Coven of Solaria was born among the celestial bodies, where the first star seeds, including Soraya's ancestors, were imbued with cosmic energy and tasked with preserving the balance of light throughout the universe.

Soraya's lineage is rich with tales of otherworldly journeys and interstellar battles, where her forebears harnessed the power of the Orion stars to combat the forces of darkness that threatened to consume not just their world but many others across the galaxy. Each generation of the Solaria coven has passed down the sacred rituals and incantations that hold the secrets of the stars, their magick a blend of cosmic energy and earthly wisdom.

As Soraya arranges the sacred crystals in a precise pattern around the altar, their facets catching the moonlight and refracting it into shimmering beams, she feels a deep connection to her star seed heritage. The symbols etched into the stones beneath her feet are not just ancient runes but stellar maps, guiding the coven in their earthly and celestial duties. The air hums with a familiar energy, a resonance that echoes the frequencies of Orion's distant stars, reminding Soraya that she is both of this earth and the stars above.

This night, as she places the Astral Sphere, an artifact passed down through generations of star seeds onto the altar, she is unaware that the ritual will awaken dormant powers within her, linking her more deeply to the cosmic forces of Orion than ever before. The full moon's light, amplified by the energy of the altar, will soon pierce the veil between worlds, setting into motion events that will challenge everything Soraya knows about her role as High Priestess and her place within the grand design of the universe.

As she arranges her sacred tools with precise care, a sense of urgency tingles in her fingertips, as if the cosmos themselves are whispering warnings into her ear. The altar, set upon a weathered boulder, emanates a radiant energy, its power amplified by the celestial crystals—amethyst, moonstone, and quartz—that shimmer with an otherworldly light. These stones have been passed down through generations of her star seed ancestors, each one imbued with the memories and magick of those who came before her.

Soraya's long black hair cascades over her shoulders, and

her eyes—a deep shade of lavender, reflecting the distant starlight of her origins—gleam with determination. Clad in a bohemian dress embroidered with wildflowers, she moves gracefully, her fingers tracing ethereal symbols through the rising smoke, her voice weaving a melodic incantation that drifts through the rustling leaves. The ancient oaks, standing as silent witnesses, seem to recognize her, their gnarled branches reaching out as if to touch the celestial power that radiates from within her.

As Soraya's incantation crescendos, a sudden gust of wind sweeps through the grove, snuffing out half the candles and plunging the altar into a dance of shadows and light. Startled, Soraya clutches at her chest, struck by an invisible force, and collapses beside her sacred space, her body still and silent upon the leaf-littered earth.

Panic ensues in the grove as her coven members rush to her side. Gideon Thatcher, her confidant and unspoken love, is first by her side, his tall figure bending protectively over her. His dark curls shadow his tear-filled gray eyes as he clasps her cold hand, his voice breaking the night's silence with a desperate plea. "Soraya, wake up! Please, come back to me," he murmurs, pressing her hand to his forehead in a gesture of profound grief and love.

Amidst the chaos, Marina stands withdrawn, her raven-black hair and sharp hazel eyes shadowed by a mix of fear and guilt. Dorian, sensing her distress, wraps an arm around her, trying to offer comfort as his own eyes search the grove for unseen threats.

In the shadowy fringes of the grove, unseen yet profoundly present, Soraya's spirit stands, her gaze fixed on a small, luminous figure that appears among the trees. Zephyr, with his opalescent eyes and twilight-hued aura, regards her with a mixture of sympathy and solemnity.

"Soraya Avalon," he intones, his voice chiming through the cool air, "the veil has been crossed."

Confusion and fear flicker across Soraya's face. "Crossed? Am I… dead?"

"Not dead, but displaced," Zephyr clarifies gently. "You've been ensnared by a curse, cast into the Moonlit Labyrinth by betrayal within your own ranks."

A cold realization dawns on Soraya, her heart heavy with the weight of this truth. "My coven… who would betray me?"

"Not all," Zephyr reassures, "but one whose heart has darkened with envy. You must navigate the labyrinth, uncover the betrayal, and reclaim your place by breaking the curse."

Soraya's resolve hardens as she looks into Zephyr's eyes, seeing not just a guide but a reflection of her own star seed lineage—a lineage that has survived trials far greater than this. "Guide me, Zephyr. I must return."

As they step together into the swirling mists of the labyrinth, Soraya's spirit is buoyed by the echoes of Gideon's vows and the cosmic energy that pulses through her being, a beacon calling her back to the world she must fight to reclaim. The journey ahead is fraught with shadows and deceit, but Soraya is ready to confront whatever the labyrinth holds, armed with her heritage, her love, and her unbreakable will.

CHAPTER 1

A CURSED RITUAL

So, I just died! I mean, I think I did. One minute I'm setting up my altar for the full moon, feeling the usual hum of cosmic energy in my veins, and now I'm standing here, watching everyone react to my body like it's a bad scene from a horror flick. WTH just happened? How'd I die? My coven—my family, my friends—wouldn't do this. And what is that sound? I turn towards the noise and see this little person waving their finger at me, beckoning like they're hailing a cab. Did I just take drugs? What is happening?

Earlier that evening, before the ritual began, I noticed Gideon Thatcher watching me from the grove's edge, his gray eyes filled with an emotion I can't quite place. Admiration? Something deeper? He's always been protective, but tonight, there was something extra in his gaze. Maybe it was the talisman he crafted for me—an intricate piece he pressed into my hand with a whisper of, "For protection." I felt a warmth in my chest when I accepted it, a brief moment that made my heart flutter even as I turned back to light the sacred fire.

But now, all that seems like a distant memory. The figure waving at me has a luminescent glow, its eyes twinkling like fireflies in the night. The forest, usually so full of life and mystery, is still bathed in moonlight, but the edges are blurred by a dense fog that swirls and shifts, making everything look like a scene from a dream—or a nightmare. My coven members are circling my lifeless body, their faces twisted in grief and confusion, like they can't believe what they're seeing.

Rowena's shoulders are heaving with sobs, her usually fierce expression crumbling under the weight of despair. Gideon is muttering incantations over my head, his voice low and frantic, trying to pull me back from wherever I've gone. Artemis, always so calm and composed, is desperately scrying into a bowl of water, her eyes wide with panic as she searches for answers in the ripples. Marina and Dorian exchange glances that scream panic, while Basil paces back and forth, his brow furrowed as he tries to make sense of the scene. They're a blur of motion and noise, and no matter how much I want to reach out and comfort them, I can't touch any of them.

Nearby, Thalia Moore stands with her eyes brimming with tears, her usual enchanting smile now a mere shadow of itself. The shimmering folds of her robes catch the firelight, but even her charm, which usually lifts everyone's spirits, seems powerless against the gravity of this moment. Finnian Hawk, still in human form, watches over the clearing like a hawk ready to strike. His dark hair is tousled, and his sharp, vigilant gaze pierces the mist as he senses the tension in the air, his primal instincts on high alert.

Celeste Foxglove, sitting cross-legged with her astral travel tools in hand, is deep in concentration. Her long, flowing hair moves around her like an ethereal aura as she whispers incantations to explore the astral plane. Her dreamy expression turns serious, her brows knitting together as she searches for the answers that might guide the coven through this darkness.

Ronan Aldridge, surrounded by glowing devices that pulse with magickal energy, is focused on blending digital tools with ancient rituals. His brow furrows in concentration, his fingers moving deftly as he creates a web of protection that will, hopefully, shield the clearing from whatever forces might be lurking.

Sylvia Marrow stands at the edge of the circle, her presence almost unnoticed as she communes with the spirits. Her quiet, enigmatic nature always kept her on the outskirts, but now her abilities are crucial. Her voice is soft, almost a whisper, as she tries to reach out to my lost spirit.

I see myself lying there, my body lifeless, at the heart of the circle. It's surreal, like watching a movie where the main character doesn't realize she's dead. My light skin still gleams in the moonlight, and my long, wavy black hair, accented with curtain bangs that delicately kiss my eyelashes, frames my face. My lavender eyes—though closed now—always held a warmth that made everyone around me feel safe. My bohemian dress, with its intricate floral embroidery, swirls around me like a tapestry of wildflowers, a reflection of my deep connection to all things earthly and celestial. Seeing myself like this, so still, so silent, leaves me feeling hollow. My aura, usually so vibrant, seems to have dimmed, and it leaves the coven reeling in disbelief.

Gideon kneels beside me, clasping my hand tightly pressing it to his forehead. He's tall, with dark, unruly curls that fall into his brooding gray eyes. Right now, those eyes are filled with grief, and tears streak down his rugged face. "Soraya Avalon, I love you," he whispers, his voice cracking with emotion. "Come back. Please come back. I need you."

Beside him, Rowena touches his shoulder gently, her platinum blonde curls wild and windblown, her freckled face red from crying. Her piercing blue eyes are swimming with tears as she reaches out to him with a trembling hand. "Gideon, what do we do?" she asks, her voice small and uncertain. She's always been the fierce one, the confident one, but right now, she looks lost.

Gideon shakes his head, his expression tortured. "Artemis, scry the path," he says, glancing up at her. "Find out where she's gone."

Artemis kneels beside the fire, the water in her scrying bowl rippling with violet light as she mutters a series of incantations. She's tall and willowy, with auburn hair braided with sprigs of thyme and lavender, and her green eyes shimmer with mystic energy. She traces symbols across the surface of the water, her brow furrowed in concentration. "I see a fog," she whispers. "A labyrinth between worlds."

Gideon closes his eyes, clutching my hand even tighter. "I know you're fighting," he murmurs. "I'll be right here when you find your way back."

Marina and Dorian exchange anxious glances. Marina's raven-black hair is cut into a sleek bob, framing her angular face, while her hazel eyes dart between the coven members, wide with panic. Dorian's silver-streaked curls hang over his forehead, and he nervously rubs at the silver rings that adorn his fingers as he tries to calm Marina with his deep, soothing voice. They grip each other's arms like lifelines, their anxiety palpable.

Basil paces back and forth, his thick brows knitted in concentration. His chestnut beard is neatly trimmed, and his bright, intelligent eyes are fixed on the ground, searching for clues. He mutters to himself, stringing together fragmented thoughts, trying to untangle the web of deceit that has ensnared their High Priestess.

I turn my attention back to the tiny figure that's still waving me toward the mist. Curiosity beats out the confusion, and I take a step toward the glowing guide.

"Hey, you!" I shout, my voice echoing strangely in the mist. "What's going on? Did I die? Am I hallucinating?"

The figure doesn't respond immediately but instead scampers deeper into the fog, its movements rhythmic, like it's conducting an invisible symphony. I follow, feeling oddly detached, like I'm floating through the mist. The forest around me grows quieter, and the light dims to a twilight hue.

Finally, the guide stops and turns to face me. He's a diminutive, enigmatic figure whose luminous aura shimmers in the mist like a beacon in the twilight. Barely reaching my waist in height, he possesses a delicate, ethereal frame cloaked in flowing robes of iridescent fabric that shifts through every shade of twilight, from dusky lavender to pale silver. The robes ripple like water in the soft breeze, trailing mist-like tendrils behind him. His hair, fine and glowing with an otherworldly shimmer, cascades down his back in a soft halo of silver light, almost obscuring the intricate patterns of glowing runes tattooed along his temples.

His eyes gleam like molten opals, swirling with hues of violet, teal, and gold that seem to hold ancient secrets and mischief in equal measure. He blinks slowly, his long, pale lashes brushing softly against his cheeks. When he moves, it's with an elegant grace that leaves trails of light in the air, as if the very fabric of reality is bending around him.

His small hands are clasped together at his chest, fingertips glowing like embers as he beckons me further into the fog, his gestures playful and rhythmic, like a conductor guiding an invisible orchestra. His voice rings out, clear and melodic, each word chiming like a silver bell and reverberating in the mist.

"Soraya Avalon, High Priestess of the Coven of Solaria," he says, tilting his head thoughtfully, "You are no longer among the living."

"What?" I blurt, eyes widening. "I can't be dead! I was in the middle of our Full Moon ritual and didn't even see anything coming."

"The curse has pulled your spirit from your mortal coil," the guide continues, his voice now tinged with a hint of solemnity. "You've been betrayed."

My stomach churns as the realization hits me. "Betrayed? By whom?"

"Someone within your own coven," the guide replies, his eyes now glinting with a knowing sadness. "The curse you inhaled was designed to cast your spirit into the Moonlit Labyrinth."

"The what?"

"The Moonlit Labyrinth," he repeats, pointing to the fog around us. "A maze between worlds where spirits wander. You have until the full moon wanes to return to your body, or your spirit will be lost here forever."

A chill races down my spine, the cold seeping into my bones. "But how? How do I get back?"

"You must journey through the labyrinth," he says. "Face the shadows that linger within and uncover the betrayal that brought you here. Only then can you break the curse."

I glance back toward the clearing, where my coven members still grieve over my body, their emotions a tangled mess of sorrow and confusion. "Who would do this to me?"

"That, you must discover," the guide says, his eyes gleaming with a mischievous glint. "But beware, the path is not straightforward. The labyrinth will test you."

I rub my temples and look back at the figure. "And who are you?"

"Your guide," he replies, offering a soft bow. "Call me Zephyr."

"All right, Zephyr, what do I do?"

"Follow me," Zephyr chirps, skipping ahead into the fog, his tiny feet barely making a sound.

As I grip my necklace—a cherished heirloom from my great-great-grandmother—I feel a surge of resolve flood through me. This necklace is more than just a piece of jewelry; it's a tangible connection to the resilient spirit of my lineage, a constant reminder of the strength that flows through my veins.

The pendant at its heart, a rare and stunning crystal only found in the rugged mountains of Massachusetts, glistens with a mesmerizing light. Named Mysticite for its unique origin, the crystal captivates with its deep amethyst hues and silver flecks that twinkle like distant stars. Shaped into an elegant teardrop and encased in a silver frame, its intricate Celtic knots symbolize the interconnectedness of all life forces, reinforcing its protective and empowering qualities.

This necklace, passed down through generations of strong women, hangs from a fine, twisted silver chain that feels almost alive against my skin. As I hold the cool, smooth crystal, I am reminded of the legacy and courage embedded in its core—empowering me to face the shadows and deception that lay ahead.

Grasping Zephyr's warm hand, I press on through the labyrinth. The fog tries to shroud my path, but Zephyr's luminous presence cuts through the gloom like a beacon, guiding me steadily forward. Each step solidifies my determination; no traitor's schemes will deter me. I will uncover the deceit, reclaim my life, and return to my coven as their High Priestess. No labyrinth or curse can hold me down; the legacy of my ancestors is with me, embodied in the ancient crystal that beats against my heart like a drum of war, echoing through the ages.

With a determined step, I plunge into the Moonlit Labyrinth, Zephyr leading the way. The stakes have never been higher—not just for me, but for the ancient legacy I carry, a legacy that stretches across time and space, connecting me to a lineage of star seeds who have fought battles far greater than this. I can feel their strength within me, a cosmic thread that binds us all, urging me to keep going, to fight for my survival, and for the preservation of a power that transcends this earthly plane.

Chapter 2

Echoes of Deceit

As we venture deeper into the labyrinth, each step resonates with an echo, swallowed by the swirling fog that clings to us like a second skin. The air grows colder, thickening like syrup, making every breath feel heavy, laden with the weight of unseen mysteries. Shadows shift along the misty walls, their tendrils curling and reaching toward me as if alive. Ahead, Zephyr glides effortlessly, his robes trailing behind him like ghostly streams of twilight. The pale light of the moon barely penetrates the labyrinth's canopy, enveloping us in a dim, eerie gloom.

"Zephyr, where exactly are we headed?" My voice cuts through the silence like a sharp twig snapping underfoot.

"The center," he replies, his chiming voice barely audible above the fog. "It is there that the first echo will reveal itself."

"Echo?" I frown, peering into the haze.

"A trace of the betrayal that cast you into this prison," Zephyr explains, slowing down to walk beside me. "This labyrinth is a reflection of your memories, twisted by the curse. Each echo represents a piece of the puzzle you must uncover."

We round a corner where tall hedges rise high, their brambles twisted like skeletal fingers. A faint whispering weaves through the branches, curling through the mist like tendrils of smoke. I tighten my grip on my necklace, following Zephyr deeper into the maze, where the path winds unpredictably.

The whispering grows louder. I catch fleeting glimpses of shadowy figures moving through the fog, their faces distorted, their voices an indistinct murmur like a long-forgotten memory. Zephyr pauses in front of a low archway covered in ivy, the tangled leaves trembling as though disturbed by an unseen breeze.

"Beyond here lies the first echo," he murmurs, gesturing toward the dark entrance. "Step forward and remember what you need."

I steel myself, brushing away a stray lock of hair, and duck beneath the archway. Inside, the mist thickens until I can hardly see my own hand. My breath tightens as the chill air presses against me, and the ground beneath my feet becomes uneven. The murmurs grow into sharp, jagged cries.

Shapes flicker before me—a memory made real yet surreal. I see my coven gathered around the altar in a dimly lit clearing, the moon casting long shadows over their familiar faces—my friends, my family. They're chanting, their voices harmonizing like a haunting melody. Yet, I notice Gideon, Rowena, Artemis, Marina, and the others, are not in harmony; their voices are discordant and broken.

Faces twist in anguish. Tears stream down Rowena's cheeks as she clutches Marina for support. Gideon's brow is furrowed in agony as he cries out an incantation. Above it all, a dark figure looms, a shadow cloaked in the fog itself, shrouding the clearing in despair. It points at me, and a whisper snakes through the night.

"High Priestess," the voice hisses, wrapping around my ears like smoke. "Beware the traitor."

As the last whispers of the echo fade into the chilling fog, a profound realization grips my heart. The vision, though fragmented and surreal, was vivid in its accusation. Marina, her posture rigid with power, stands at the forefront of the vision. Her shadow stretches unnaturally long across the moonlit clearing, merging with the darkness that swells around the edges of the coven. In her hand, she clenches a talisman—a serpent coiled around a moonstone, a symbol known only to the highest echelons of our order, and one that Marina should not possess.

"Zephyr," I begin, my voice a mix of disbelief and dawning horror, "I saw her with the serpent-moon talisman. The one that went missing from the sanctum last winter."

Zephyr's face, usually an unreadable mask of ancient wisdom, tightens slightly. "That talisman was meant to safeguard the deepest secrets of our lineage," he murmurs, a storm brewing in his ageless eyes. "Only a few knew of its hiding place, and fewer still could retrieve it without arousing suspicion."

The fog around us seems to thicken, reflecting my turmoil. "It's Marina," I confess, the words tasting bitter on my tongue. "She must have taken it, using its power to twist the labyrinth's magick for her own ends."

Zephyr nods slowly, his hand firm in mine. "It's a dark path she's chosen. The talisman's power is great, but the ancient laws of our realm bind it. It reveals its bearer to those who truly look.

Marina may not realize that her betrayal has left traces, echoes in the very fabric of this place, visible only to those who share a connection with the labyrinth's core."

"Then that's what I saw—the talisman's echo, showing me the truth behind the shadows," I say, newfound resolve lifting the weight from my shoulders. "She's manipulating the labyrinth's energy, bending its paths to hide her steps."

We move deeper into the maze, the mist parting reluctantly before Zephyr's ethereal light. Each step forward is a step toward uncovering the depths of Marina's deception, toward a confrontation that I both dread and desire. Marina, once my sister in the craft, now my darkest adversary, waits in the heart of the labyrinth, surrounded by the twisted magick she has summoned.

"To find her, to face her, we must unravel the labyrinth's darkest paths," Zephyr states, his voice echoing slightly off the ancient stone walls. "Prepare yourself, Soraya. The heart of the maze holds more than echoes; it holds the truths we are often afraid to face."

With each twist and turn, each chilling revelation, I steel myself for the inevitable. The shadows may play tricks, and the moonlight may barely reach, but with Zephyr by my side, I am ready to confront the darkness, to bring Marina's treachery into the light.

I take his hand, and together we walk deeper into the fog. The mist wraps around us like a shroud, but Zephyr's glow cuts through, guiding me forward. My breath forms soft tendrils as I follow his lead, my eyes fixed on the shifting shadows along the twisted hedges.

The labyrinth seems to come alive around us, its pathways

shifting like the coils of a serpent. Walls sprout where there were none, and paths vanish without a trace. The maze twists and loops back on itself, the hedges pressing in close, the mist clinging like a second skin. Zephyr keeps one step ahead, his luminous robes trailing through the fog like ghostly tendrils, his voice echoing softly through the haze.

"Be careful, Soraya Avalon," he warns, glancing back at me over his shoulder. "The labyrinth can twist your senses and deceive your eyes."

"Why was the Moonlit Labyrinth created?" I ask, my voice cutting through the eerie quiet.

"It has always existed," Zephyr replies, his voice like the rustling of leaves. "A place between worlds, where the shadows of the past linger. It is both a sanctuary and a prison."

I nod, though uncertainty churns within me. My grip tightens on my necklace as the fog thickens around us, the shadows shifting and merging into indistinct shapes. Somewhere in the distance, I hear the soft hum of chanting, and the air ripples with dark energy.

We step into a clearing, and I take a breath, feeling the cool air swirl around me. At the center stands a towering oak, its branches spreading wide like the outstretched fingers of a giant. Beneath its canopy, twisted shadows slither across the ground, writhing like serpents in the dim moonlight.

"Another echo lies here," Zephyr whispers, gesturing toward the tree. "It will show you the way."

I approach cautiously, peering into the shadows beneath the tree's canopy. The fog curls around me, and the ground trembles beneath my feet. My breath catches as a flicker of light shines through the mist, and the air hums with energy. Images form in the shadows, and I see glimpses of Marina in the clearing, her face twisted in anger as she raises her hand toward me.

Her words reach me as a faint whisper, like the hiss of distant thunder. "She will lead us to ruin," she mutters. "Soraya Avalon must fall."

The echo fades, and the shadows vanish into the fog. I swallow hard, turning back to Zephyr, my heart racing.

"Do you see now?" Zephyr asks softly. "The shadows speak the truth."

"Yes," I murmur. "But I still need to find the source of her darkness."

"Then we must continue," Zephyr says, extending his hand.

With renewed determination, I take his hand and follow him back into the labyrinth, my resolve growing with each step. The fog closes in behind us, the shadows melting into the night as we plunge deeper into the maze.

We walk for what feels like hours, the twisted paths curving and looping as if designed to disorient. The fog swirls around us like living tendrils, reaching out to brush against my skin and blur my senses. The walls of the labyrinth shift, occasionally revealing shadowy figures that whisper threats and taunts before vanishing back into the mist. I try to keep my eyes fixed on Zephyr's glowing outline ahead, but the fog wraps around me so tightly that the faintest glimmer of his robes is my only anchor.

Finally, the air hums with new energy, and Zephyr pauses, pointing ahead toward a narrow archway covered in winding ivy. "The second echo is here," he says softly.

I steel myself and step through, the mist curling around my ankles like ethereal chains. On the other side, the air grows colder, and my breath crystallizes in the twilight chill. Shapes shift before me, blurry and distorted like a reflection in rippling water. My fingers clench around my necklace, and I mutter a quick prayer to the Goddess.

"Goddess of the moonlit paths, guide me through the shadows. Grant me clarity and protect me from deceit."

With this invocation, I feel a subtle warmth spreading through me, bolstering my courage as I face the shifting illusions of the labyrinth.

The fog parts, revealing another memory made real. I see my coven gathered around a fire in the clearing, their faces lit with warm, amber light as they chant softly in harmony. But something feels off. The air hums with an undercurrent of tension, and shadows twist at the edge of the firelight.

Gideon's voice rises, his gray eyes glowing in the flickering flames as he calls out an incantation. Rowena stands beside him, her platinum curls framing her freckled face as she adds her own voice to the chant. Basil murmurs softly under his breath, his chestnut beard twitching as he traces protective sigils into the earth. Dorian paces back and forth, his silver-streaked curls brushing his forehead as he grips his dagger, his hazel eyes darting toward the shadows that twist and coil at the edge of the grove.

Thalia stands nearby, her flowing robes adorned with intricate patterns and earthy hues, dancing playfully around her as she raises her voice in melodic incantations. Her purpose is clear: to soothe the tension within the coven. Her words carry both charm and wit, weaving a protective web around her fellow members.

Meanwhile, Finnian, a guardian in wolf form, patrols the perimeter of the clearing. His primal instincts guide him, sharp senses attuned to any disturbance. His watchful eyes scan the darkness, ensuring the safety of the sacred circle. The moonlight glints off his sleek fur, emphasizing his silent vigilance.

Celeste kneels beside the fire, her eyes closed in deep concentration as she mutters softly to herself, navigating the astral plane in search of hidden truths. Ronan works quietly, weaving technomancy spells into the protective circle to bolster their defenses with a blend of digital and arcane energy. Sylvia stands at the edge, her shadowy presence barely noticeable as she whispers incantations that allow her to commune with the spirit world.

And there, just beyond the flickering light, is Marina, her face twisted in fury as she watches the others. Her raven-black hair falls across her angular face, and her hazel eyes burn with an intensity that chills me to the core. Her lips move in a silent incantation, and her shadow stretches across the clearing like a serpent, its tendrils curling toward the fire.

A whisper snakes through the night, coiling around my ears like smoke. "The High Priestess must fall," the voice hisses, winding through the fog like a phantom breeze. "The grove will be ours."

My heart races as the vision blurs, and the fog swirls around me once more, leaving me alone in the mist. I stumble back, breath hitching in my throat as I turn to Zephyr, who stands just beyond the archway, his luminous gaze fixed on me.

"The echoes reveal the shadows," Zephyr murmurs softly. "The labyrinth holds the truth."

"But why?" I murmur, my voice barely above a whisper. "Why would she betray me?"

Zephyr's eyes gleam faintly in the twilight as he extends his hand toward me. "The labyrinth twists the paths," he says. "To uncover the truth, you must journey deeper."

With a deep breath, I take Zephyr's hand, his fingers warm against mine. The fog wraps around us like a shroud, but Zephyr's glow cuts through it, guiding me forward with each determined step. My breath forms soft wisps as I follow his lead, my eyes fixed on the shifting shadows along the twisted hedges.

The labyrinth folds back upon itself, its pathways growing increasingly narrow, as if they seek to ensnare me. Mist envelops me, thick and unyielding, while whispers from unseen specters heckle from the shadows. My eyes remain locked on Zephyr, his figure illuminated and ethereal, his robes billowing like threads of twilight. His voice, a melodious echo, drifts softly through the dense air.

Finally, we reach another clearing, and Zephyr pauses, his eyes gleaming brightly in the dim moonlight. "This is the third echo," he murmurs softly. "The shadow of deceit."

I step forward cautiously, my fingers curling around my necklace as I peer into the swirling mist. The ground hums with energy, and the fog parts to reveal another memory made real.

The grove is dimly lit, the moon hanging low in the sky as the coven gathers in a circle around a twisted oak. Their faces are twisted in anguish as they chant softly in harmony, their voices tinged with fear and uncertainty. My own voice joins theirs, but I can't see myself in the clearing. Instead, I hover above like a phantom, watching as Gideon clasps my hand tightly and presses his forehead against my knuckles.

"Please, Soraya," he murmurs, his gray eyes brimming with tears. "Come back."

Rowena stands beside him, her shoulders heaving with sobs

as she clutches Marina's arm for support. Artemis kneels beside the fire, her auburn hair woven with sprigs of thyme and lavender as she peers into her scrying bowl. Basil traces protective sigils into the earth, his chestnut beard twitching as he mutters incantations under his breath.

Dorian paces nervously, gripping his dagger with determination, while Thalia whispers a playful chant, hoping to encourage her coven members. Finnian prowls around the clearing as a panther, his luminous green eyes scanning for danger. Celeste hums softly in her trance, her gaze fixed on the astral plane, while Ronan's intricate network of technomancy spells glimmers around the circle. Sylvia, her shadowy presence barely noticeable, communes with the spirit world, seeking guidance.

But beyond the flickering firelight stands a shadowy figure cloaked in darkness, their eyes gleaming with malevolence. They raise their hand toward the twisted oak, and a whisper snakes through the night like smoke.

"The grove will fall," the voice hisses, winding around the clearing like a serpent. "The High Priestess must be cast down."

The shadowy figure retreats into the mist, their laughter echoing softly through the fog. The coven's chanting falters, and their voices grow discordant and strained as they struggle to maintain harmony.

The vision fades, and the fog swirls around me once more. I stumble back, breath hitching in my throat as I turn to Zephyr, who stands just beyond the clearing, his luminous gaze fixed on me.

"The labyrinth holds the truth," he murmurs softly. "The shadows of deceit."

I swallow hard and take Zephyr's hand, his fingers warm against mine as we walk deeper into the labyrinth. My resolve grows with each step, my breath forming soft wisps in the chill air as the fog wraps around us like a shroud.

The labyrinth may twist its paths, but the truth will be revealed. The shadows of betrayal would not hold me back. I will uncover the traitor who cast me into this maze, and I will return to my coven as High Priestess.

In the labyrinth's heart, where shadows play tricks and the moonlight scarcely reaches, I grapple with the Shadows of Deceit. Zephyr, my guide, leads me through the misty corridors with a firm, guiding hand. The air is thick with the scent of damp earth and ancient magic, the fog swirling around us like a living entity.

As we approach a clearer part of the labyrinth, I hear the faint strains of a powerful chant, echoing through the gloom. It's Gideon's voice, filled with raw emotional intensity, that sends shivers down my spine. He stands before the sacred fire, his figure bathed in its flickering golden light, chanting with a fierce determination that speaks of deep-seated love and desperate hope.

Rowena and Artemis are there too, standing hand in hand, their voices melding together in a harmonious incantation. Their words are a protective shroud, weaving through the air with the power to fend off the encroaching shadows. In a rare moment of vulnerability beneath the moon's watchful gaze, they share a kiss —a promise of mutual support and undying loyalty in the face of the darkness that seeks to engulf us all.

I step closer, drawn by the scene of unity and strength and by Gideon's unwavering resolve to restore what was lost. The coven's energy pulsates through the clearing, a beacon of hope that fights back against the stifling darkness of the labyrinth.

Zephyr whispers beside me, his voice a soothing balm in the chilling air, "See how they rally around the fire, Soraya. This is the strength of your coven, the power of hearts united against a common foe."

Moved by the scene, I add my voice to theirs, speaking the words that have come to define our quest:

Gideon's Chant: "Exorior ex umbra, lux perpetua luceat!" His voice cuts through the darkness, a call for light to dispel the shadows.

Rowena and Artemis's Incantation: "Protegamus et custodiamus, semitas nostras claras servemus!" Their words knit the air into a shield, guarding our path from the lurking darkness.

Sylvia's Closing Incantation: "Ultima vincula frangimus, pacem redintegramus!"

With a solemn tone, she seals our ritual, her words a binding force that seeks to mend the fractured peace.

The sacred fire blazes up, its flames leaping towards the sky as if reaching for the stars themselves. The shadows recoil, beaten back by the surge of collective power that resonates through the clearing.

With a deep breath, I feel the weight of the past and the promise of the future converge in this moment. The labyrinth around us seems to hold its breath, the eternal dance of light and shadow pausing in reverence of our resolve.

Gideon turns to my lifeless body, his eyes gleaming with tears of relief and a fire born of renewed hope. "We will find her," he vows, his voice steady despite the emotion that thickens it. "Together, we will bring Soraya back from the shadows."

As the incantations fade into the night, leaving a resonant silence in their wake, I know that this is but one step in our journey. The path ahead is fraught with challenges, and the Shadows of Deceit lie deep. But with my coven by my side, each step is a strike against the darkness, each chant a beacon lighting our way back home.

Chapter 3

The Shroud of Betrayal

The night envelops the grove in a cold embrace, its tendrils thick and chilling, like the breath of an ancient beast. I meld into the darkness, a shadow among shadows, as if I were always a part of this creeping gloom. My heart hammers—not with fear, but with a tumultuous blend of exhilaration and regret. I watch the chaos unfold from my concealed spot among the twisted oaks, my breath barely stirring the air. The fire at the center of the clearing casts flickering shadows that dance devilishly on the faces of my former brethren, now swept up in a tempest of fear and confusion.

"Soraya!" Gideon's anguished cry pierces the night, echoing off the trees as he cradles her fallen form. His face is a mask of desperate sorrow, every line etched with the raw pain of loss. The others huddle around, their faces twisted with panic and disbelief. Their unity—once something I envied—is now a bitter reminder of what I never truly had.

My eyes linger on Gideon, the pain in his gaze reflecting a

love so deep it stings. "What sorcery is this?" he bellows, his voice trembling with a mix of rage and despair. His gaze sweeps the clearing, his eyes narrowing as they briefly skim the shadows where I lurk.

"Marina, what have you done?" Artemis steps forward, her voice sharp, slicing through the still air with the weight of her accusation. The silver light of the moon casts an ethereal glow on her face, highlighting the fierce determination in her eyes.

"I've taken back what should have been mine all along," I reply, my voice steady, though the storm inside me rages on. "Our ancestors were wronged, cast aside—this coven's legacy tainted by ignorance and exclusion."

Rowena, her eyes wide with a mix of fear and anger, steps up beside Artemis. "You speak of exclusion," she spits, her voice shaking, "yet you sought to erase Soraya entirely? How is that any different?"

"Our heritage demanded justice," I snap back, feeling the ancient fire of our ancestors burning within me. "You all basked in her light, blind to the shadows she cast over my rightful place."

Dorian, ever the voice of reason, moves forward cautiously, his gaze filled with wariness. "Marina, this isn't you. This… hatred, this darkness—it's not who you were. We were your family."

"Family?" The word drips with bitterness as it leaves my lips. "A family that glorifies one while diminishing others because of old bloodlines? I was never truly one of you. Today, I reclaim what is mine by birthright."

The words hang in the air, heavy with the weight of generations of pain and betrayal. They don't know the full story, the dark secrets buried deep in our shared past. They see only the present, the immediate consequences of my actions, but they are blind to the roots of my anger, the deep injustice that has festered for centuries.

My lineage is one of power and pride, stretching back to the earliest days of this coven. My ancestors, the true guardians of this grove, were once revered for their wisdom and strength. But all that changed during the dark days of the Salem witch trials. Fear and suspicion swept through the land like a plague, turning friend against friend, family against family. In that frenzy, my ancestors were betrayed, cast out, and their legacy erased from the coven's history.

The betrayal didn't end there. Even after the trials, when the survivors regrouped and rebuilt, the shadow of that treachery loomed large. My family was never fully welcomed back into the fold, always kept on the periphery, our rightful place usurped by those who had betrayed us. The bloodlines that were once intertwined with power and respect were now seen as tainted, cursed, an uncomfortable reminder of the coven's dark past.

But I know the truth. I've spent years uncovering the secrets hidden in old grimoires and whispered through the generations of my family. The power that once flowed through our veins has not been lost—it has been lying dormant, waiting for someone strong enough to reclaim it.

The others in the grove don't understand. They see only the actions I've taken, the immediate consequences, and they judge me for it. But they are blind to the injustice that has festered for centuries, the deep wound that has never truly healed. They see me as the villain in this story, but I know that I am the hero—one who must take on the burden of righting a wrong that has lingered for too long.

As they process my words, a heavy silence falls over the grove, broken only by the crackling of the fire and the whisper of the wind through the trees. My attention shifts back to the labyrinthine path I must follow. With every whispered accusation and desperate plea from behind me, I feel the pull of the darkness grow stronger, drawing me deeper into its embrace.

"Wait!" Sylvia's voice, usually calm and steady, is tinged with desperation as she approaches. "Marina, think about what you're doing and the harmony we've achieved as a coven. This isn't the way to set things right."

"Harmony?" I scoff, my laugh hollow as it mingles with the rustling leaves around us. "There is no harmony in suppression. There is no peace in being cast aside. I seek balance, one that honors all, not just the favored few."

Before they can respond, I begin to chant softly, invoking an ancient spell that wraps me in shadows—a cloak woven from the dark essence of the labyrinth itself. "Umbrae, ad me venite," I murmur, feeling the power of the words as they take hold. The shadows respond, wrapping around me, dimming the light, muffling the sounds of the grove.

As the spell takes hold, I begin to fade from their sight, like a ghost retreating into the mist. The voices behind me grow fainter, their calls laced with betrayal and sorrow, but I don't look back.

The labyrinth awaits, its paths coiled like the serpents of my ancestors' will. Here, in the darkness, I will forge my destiny and reshape the legacy of this coven. My steps are sure, my heart alight with a dark purpose as I navigate the twisted, shifting paths.

Each turn draws me deeper into the heart of the maze, where power and secrets lie buried beneath layers of deceit and ancient magic. The air grows cooler, the mist thicker, as if the labyrinth itself breathes with me, whispering its hidden truths in my ear.

The shadows cling to me, their whispers guiding my way. They speak of power, hidden doors and forgotten rites. I listen, my resolve hardening with each whispered secret. This path, born of shadows and betrayal, is mine to tread. In its depths lies not just the reclamation of a lost legacy, but the reshaping of our world's very foundation.

As dawn approaches, the first light filters through the dense canopy, casting a pale, ghostly glow on the path ahead. It is here, in the convergence of light and shadow, that I will make my stand, rewrite the history that has bound us, and finally step into the light that was denied to me—not as Marina, but as Marina the Reclaimer, the Restorer of the Forgotten Balance.

I prepare myself to face what lies ahead, the labyrinth pulsing with anticipation, as if it, too, is ready to unveil its deepest secrets. With the ancient incantations of my ancestors on my lips, I am ready to confront whatever the labyrinth holds to claim the power that is rightfully mine.

The whispers of the labyrinth grow louder, echoing in the corners of my mind as I step deeper into the maze. The air is thick with anticipation, the shadows shifting restlessly, as if they sense the impending storm. I take a deep breath, steeling myself for the trials ahead. My heart beats steadily, its rhythm syncing with the pulse of the labyrinth. I know that every step I take brings me closer to the truth, closer to the power that has been hidden from me for too long.

This is my path, my destiny. No longer will I stand in the

shadows, cast aside and forgotten. I will rise from the darkness, reclaim what is mine, and reshape the world in my image. The labyrinth may be treacherous, its paths twisted and deceptive, but I am more than a match for its challenges. I am Marina the Reclaimer, the Restorer of Balance, and I will not be denied.

With one final glance back at the grove, where the last remnants of my former life flicker and fade in the firelight, I turn my face toward the labyrinth and step boldly into its depths, ready to face whatever lies ahead.

Chapter 4

Shadows of the Abyssal Chasm

Zephyr's steady glow guides me through the labyrinth's twisting corridors, his luminous robes trailing behind him like a guiding beacon in the murky haze. The fog clings to us, dense and suffocating, as if the very air conspires to trap us within its grasp. With each step, the atmosphere grows heavier, charged with a palpable energy that crackles like static in the dim moonlight.

Gideon's voice resonates in my mind, his chants echoing through the sacred grove as he leads the coven in a powerful ritual around the fire. His devotion to me—his High Priestess—is evident in every syllable, his voice trembling with emotion as he pours his soul into the incantations. The flames flicker, casting long, dancing shadows over the grove, while the other coven members join their voices with his, creating a harmonious symphony of magick that seeks to reach me in the depths of the labyrinth.

Rowena and Artemis exchange a glance filled with resolve and urgency. Their hands clasp tightly together as they whisper protective incantations, their voices intertwining like a well-practiced duet. This night, the air around them feels different, charged with an energy that has been brewing beneath the surface for countless moons. The trials they've faced together have drawn them closer, revealing a mutual respect that has quietly blossomed into something more. Under the watchful gaze of the moon, they share a tender kiss, sealing their bond with a warmth that momentarily pauses the world around them.

I feel a stir of joy within me as I witness this from afar, a gentle happiness that surprises me with its intensity. Rowena and Artemis are perfect for each other; their strengths complement each other, like the night balances the day. Their union, I know, will bring a powerful alliance to the coven, a personal victory for them, and a beacon of hope for us all.

"Where are we headed next?" I ask Zephyr, my voice cutting through the stillness like a blade.

"The Abyssal Chasm," Zephyr replies softly, his words carrying a weight that settles in the pit of my stomach. "The echoes have shown you the shadow of deceit, but to uncover the full scope of Marina's betrayal, we must pass through the darkness that guards the truth."

"The Abyssal Chasm?" I repeat, a thread of uncertainty winding through my resolve.

"A place where shadows writhe and curses take root," Zephyr explains, his voice echoing through the fog. "A rift within the labyrinth where the darkest energies of betrayal fester. The chasm will test you, but you must face it to move forward."

My breath turns to wisps in the chilly air as we approach a jagged archway woven from twisted branches and thorny vines. The mist thickens, swirling around us like sentient tendrils, and the air hums with an otherworldly resonance. Zephyr steps through the archway first, his robes glowing faintly as he beckons me forward.

As I step into the abyssal gloom, the air turns frigid, unnaturally still, as if the very breath of the forest has been sucked away. My heart pounds, a rapid drumbeat echoing in my chest as my fingers tighten reflexively around my necklace, its warmth a comforting contrast to the creeping cold. The fog before me parts like curtains unveiling a sinister stage, revealing the Abyssal Chasm stretching into an endless void—a terrifying gash in the earth that seethes with malice.

Beneath me, the ground trembles, a subtle but unsettling reminder of the chasm's living presence. Shadowy figures writhe in the depths below, their distorted silhouettes a grim testament to the curse's reach, painting a macabre scene of suffering and despair.

Zephyr's voice, calm yet urgent, breaks the eerie silence. He points to the chasm's darkened expanse, his eyes reflecting the abyss. "This is the Abyssal Chasm," he murmurs. "It stands between you and the truth, twisted into a barrier of deceit by Marina's dark will. It seeks to consume those who dare cross."

I inch closer to the edge, my breath clouding in the icy air, the mist at my feet coiling like spectral chains. "How do we cross this?" My voice, though quiet, carries the weight of the challenge before me.

Zephyr produces a small silver vial from the folds of his

robes, its contents shimmering like liquid moonlight. "The shadows here twist reality, ensnaring your senses in illusions. This potion," he hands it to me, "will allow you to see through the darkness."

I uncork the vial, the herbal scent of lavender and sage wafting up to greet me, grounding me in the familiar. I take a tentative sip, warmth spreading through my body like a soothing balm, piercing the cold that clings to my bones. As the fog before my eyes clears, a path reveals itself—faintly glowing, winding through the darkness below.

Zephyr steps onto the path, his robes catching the nonexistent wind. "Follow me," he beckons, his silhouette a beacon in the encroaching gloom.

Cautiously, I step forward, the path solid underfoot yet seemingly fragile, suspended over an abyss that promises oblivion with every misstep. Each echo of my footsteps rings out sharply, a stark reminder of the vast emptiness that surrounds us. The chasm walls loom close, their damp surfaces reflecting distorted shadows as the mist tries to reclaim its hold, swirling around us like a living entity.

Zephyr's voice drifts back to me, a steady thread in the enveloping darkness. "Stay close. The shadows here are seductive, whispering lies meant to lead you astray."

His warning comes just as the whispers intensify, a cacophony of hisses and murmurs scratching at the edges of my mind, seeking entry. I focus on the light emanating from Zephyr's glow, my lifeline in this oppressive darkness. "I won't let them deceive me," I assert, my voice stronger now, fortified by the potion and my resolve.

As the path gradually widens, the oppressive atmosphere begins to lift, and we emerge into a more open space. The air shifts, charged with a new energy, different from anything I've felt before. It's as if the very ground beneath my feet hums with a power I can't quite place, something ancient and full of secrets yet to be uncovered.

Relief floods through me, and I release a breath I hadn't realized I'd been holding. Zephyr glances back at me with a nod of approval. "You've braved the Abyssal Chasm," he acknowledges, a note of respect in his tone. "Few can tread this path without faltering."

"What awaits us now?" I ask, peering into the fading mist, the sense of foreboding slowly ebbing away. My curiosity is piqued by the strange energy that surrounds us, and I can't shake the feeling that something significant lies ahead.

"Beyond here is something you need to see," Zephyr explains, his gaze fixed on the horizon where the first light of dawn begins to break through. "There's a place known as the Celestial Tower. Within its ancient walls are grimoires that hold the power to break your curse and unravel the secrets that bind you."

Grasping Zephyr's hand, I feel a renewed sense of purpose surge through me. Together, we press on, the tower's ancient knowledge drawing us forward. The shadows may linger, a dark veil trailing in our wake, but I am Soraya Emerald Avalon, and I am not alone. With each step, the truth comes nearer, and soon, I will return to my coven, armed with the knowledge and power to dispel the darkness that threatens to consume us all.

As the first rays of dawn pierce through the dense canopy,

casting long beams of light onto our path, I feel the labyrinth's grip loosening, the shadows retreating in the face of the coming day. The Celestial Tower looms ahead, its spires reaching toward the heavens, promising the answers I seek.

With Zephyr by my side and the wisdom of the ancients within reach, I step boldly forward, ready to face whatever trials lie ahead. The labyrinth may be full of shadows, but with each step, I carry the light of truth within me, a beacon guiding me back to where I belong.

As we draw closer to the Celestial Tower, I can feel the ancient magick emanating from its walls, a pulse of energy that seems to resonate with my very soul. The air around us hums with power, as if the tower itself is alive, waiting for us to uncover its secrets. The path ahead is steep, the terrain rugged and challenging, but with Zephyr's unwavering guidance and the Astral Sphere glowing steadily in my hand, I know that I have the strength to continue.

The trees around us begin to thin, revealing the tower in all its towering glory. Its stone walls are etched with runes that glow faintly in the early morning light, their intricate patterns telling tales of forgotten magicks and ancient rites. The tower's entrance, a massive archway carved from gleaming moonstone, beckons us forward, promising answers to the questions that have haunted me for so long.

Zephyr pauses at the threshold, his hand resting on the cool stone as he turns to me. "Beyond these doors lies the knowledge you seek," he says, his voice soft but filled with conviction. "But be warned, Soraya—what you find within may change everything you know about your past, and about the coven."

I meet his gaze, the weight of his words settling over me like a heavy cloak. "I'm ready," I reply, my voice steady despite the uncertainty that churns in my gut. "Whatever truths the tower holds, I'm prepared to face them."

With a nod, Zephyr pushes open the heavy doors, and together we step into the Celestial Tower, ready to unravel the mysteries within and reclaim the power that is rightfully mine.

CHAPTER 5

THE CELESTIAL TOWER'S LIGHT

The fog wraps around us like a cocoon as we continue along the twisting path, the weight of the journey pressing down on my shoulders. Zephyr's luminous robes ripple softly in the dim light, casting faint shadows on the winding hedges that line our trail. The air grows warmer, and my breath no longer forms mist in the twilight chill, a small comfort in the ever-present uncertainty of the labyrinth.

Ahead, the path widens, and a soft glow begins to pierce the fog, revealing the outline of a towering citadel against the starry night. The Celestial Tower stands before us, its ethereal spires stretching toward the moonlit sky like fingers reaching for the stars. Ancient runes shimmer along the stone walls, pulsing with a soft violet light that hums through the air like a heartbeat.

"This is the Celestial Tower," Zephyr intones softly, gesturing toward the looming structure. His voice carries a reverence that resonates within me, filling the air with a sense of awe. He points to the arched entrance, carved from moonstone, which hums with a distant melody—a forgotten tune that echoes through time. Flanking the archway are twin statues: one an ancient sage with eyes closed in deep contemplation, the other a fierce celestial beast with wings outstretched, guarding the threshold with eternal vigilance.

As we cross the threshold, the atmosphere shifts instantly. A grand hall opens up before us, bathed in silvery moonlight filtering through unseen windows. The walls are adorned with expansive tapestries that depict cosmic events—the birth of stars, the dance of planets, the weaving of fate by unseen hands. The air is thick with the scent of aged parchment mingled with the sweet, heady aroma of incense, infusing the space with a sense of ancient wisdom. The floor beneath our feet is cool, polished marble, etched with constellations that subtly shift as we move, guiding us deeper into the tower's enigmatic heart.

Spiral staircases wind upward on either side, carved from the same moonstone as the entrance, each step imbued with celestial energy as it ascends into the darkness above. Silver sconces line the walls, holding flickering candles whose flames cast elongated, dancing shadows that seem to guard against the tower's darker secrets.

Zephyr leads the way, his figure bathed in the soft glow of the moonlight as he speaks, "Within these walls lies the knowledge needed to break the curse. Each tome, each rune holds a piece of the puzzle that is your destiny."

We move forward, drawn deeper into the tower's core, surrounded by the whispers of those who sought knowledge before us. Their voices linger in the air, a chorus of wisdom and warnings, woven into the very fabric of this place.

"What exactly are we looking for?" I ask, my voice echoing off the stone walls.

"Not a book or a scroll," Zephyr replies, his chiming voice soft but sure. "But the Luminous Crown, a circlet of silver and stardust that channels celestial energies. With it, you can amplify the power of the Celestial Circle—the heart of this grove that we've drawn from for centuries."

I pause, glancing around at the familiar trees and the earth beneath my feet. The grove has always been a sanctuary, a place of gathering and protection, but the name—the Celestial Circle—feels new, like an ancient truth only now coming to light. "The Celestial Circle?" I repeat, the words feeling both foreign and inevitable on my tongue.

Zephyr nods, his eyes gleaming with an understanding far beyond my own. "It's what this place was always meant to be—a conduit of celestial power. We've all felt it, but now, with the Luminous Crown, you can fully awaken it. Only then can we hope to stand against Marina's darkness and protect what we've built here."

As I follow Zephyr up the spiraling staircase, the stone steps echo beneath our feet, each sound a drumbeat rising through the tower's heart. The air grows colder as we ascend, wrapping its chill fingers around us like a spectral cloak. I tighten my grip on my necklace, the crystal cool against my skin, and I whisper a quick incantation to steady my racing pulse:

"Guiding spirits, hush the storm,

Still my heart and keep me warm.

Light the path where shadows dwell,

Safeguard my ascent with your protective spell."

With each word, a gentle warmth spreads from the pendant,

calming the storm inside me and steadying my breath. The stone beneath my feet pulses in rhythm with my newfound calm, guiding me upward, deeper into the mysteries that await.

At the top of the staircase lies a small chamber, illuminated by a dim silver light that filters through narrow windows. Shelves line the walls, filled with scrolls and leather-bound volumes, their pages yellowed with age. In the center of the room stands a stone pedestal, its surface carved with symbols that glow softly in the twilight. Resting atop the pedestal is a circlet—the Luminous Crown—gleaming with a soft, ethereal light. Tiny stars seem to dance along the silver band, their light twinkling like distant constellations.

"The Luminous Crown," Zephyr whispers, his gaze fixed on the circlet. "Its power will amplify the energies of the Celestial Circle, allowing you to shield the grove from Marina's darkness."

I step forward cautiously, the stone cool beneath my fingertips as I reach for the circlet. The metal is smooth and warm, and as I lift it from the pedestal, faint tendrils of light spiral around my fingers like threads of stardust, filling me with a sense of purpose.

Zephyr steps beside me, his luminous gaze locked onto the circlet. "You must channel the energies of the stars through the crown," he explains, his voice resonating in the hushed air of the tower. "Focus your intention, and let the starlight protect your coven."

I close my eyes, the warmth of the crown radiating through me as I draw a deep, steadying breath. My fingers tighten around the circlet, and I begin to chant, each word a soft hum vibrating through the silvery air:

"By the light of stars above,

Bind our circle with threads of love.

Guide this spell where shadows play,

Let our strength light the way."

The air around us shivers with newfound energy, as if the very tower itself responds to my call. The runes on the pedestal glow brighter, their arcane symbols casting faint wisps of light into the chamber, swirling like smoke caught in a gentle breeze.

In the midst of the glowing runes, visions begin to form in the mist—ethereal and fluid. I see the faces of my coven gathered around the sacred fire in the grove. Moonlight bathes their features, casting an otherworldly glow on their determined faces. Rowena's platinum curls flutter in a gentle breeze, Gideon's gray eyes reflect the fire's flickering light with unwavering resolve. On the edge of the circle, Marina stands, her sharp gaze locked onto the shifting shadows, her expression twisting with fury as my spell, carried by the crown's power, weaves through the night, connecting us across the distance with a bond forged in starlight and magic.

The circlet hums with energy, and I reach out, my voice joining theirs in harmony as we weave the incantation. Light pours from the Luminous Crown, swirling around me like a vortex as the grove begins to fade into the mist. The darkness trembles, and Marina's shadow falters, her power crumbling beneath the starlight as it burns away the fog of her deception.

The grove glows brightly, the shadows retreating into the night as the coven's chanting fills the air. Marina's twisted incantation crumbles under the weight of our combined magic, her grip on the grove loosening as the light envelops her, stripping away the darkness she had cloaked herself in.

With a final word, "Solvo," which means, "I free," the

incantation fades, and the grove is bathed in a serene, silver light. My breath catches as the Luminous Crown dims, its power spent, the starlight fading from the chamber.

"You have broken the veil," Zephyr says softly, his luminous gaze still fixed on the circlet. "The curse is lifted, and your coven awaits you."

I clutch the Luminous Crown tightly, turning to Zephyr, my pulse racing with renewed determination. "The darkness will not hold me back," I murmur, my voice strong and resolute. "I will reclaim my place among my coven."

Zephyr smiles faintly, offering his hand. His fingers are warm against mine as we descend the staircase together. The fog wraps around us once more, but Zephyr's glow cuts through it, guiding me forward with each step. The path ahead is clear, and the grove awaits, its fire burning brightly in the moonlight.

With the Luminous Crown in hand and the Celestial Tower behind me, I am ready to navigate the labyrinth's final twists, reunite with my coven, and return as High Priestess. The labyrinth may still hold challenges, but with each step, I carry the light of truth and the power of the stars within me, a beacon that will guide me back to where I belong.

As we descend, the tower's ancient whispers follow the echo of the stars' blessings a constant reminder of the power now in my grasp. I feel the pull of my coven, their collective energy beckoning me home, where I am needed, where I am loved. The grove will be my sanctuary once again, but this time, with the Luminous Crown's light guiding us all, the darkness will find no purchase in our sacred circle.

CHAPTER 6

PATH THROUGH THE WYRD WOODS

Leaving the Celestial Tower behind, Zephyr's glow guides our way through the labyrinth, casting shifting shadows on the mist-covered ground. The fog, dense and almost suffocating, clings to us like a shroud. I clutch the Luminous Crown tightly in my hands, its warmth a comfort against the chill that still lingers in the air. The path twists and curves beneath my feet, a serpentine route that seems to have no end.

As we press on, the mist begins to thin, revealing a towering canopy of ancient trees bathed in spectral moonlight. Their gnarled branches stretch high above, intertwining like skeletal fingers to form a dense archway that plunges the forest floor into an eerie gloom. A faint breeze stirs the leaves, filling the air with a whisper that sends a shiver down my spine, as if the very forest is alive and watching.

"The Wyrd Woods," Zephyr murmurs, his voice a soft echo that blends with the rustling leaves. "A forest where shadows linger, and ancient magick guards the land."

I step cautiously onto the forest floor, the leaves crunching softly underfoot. The branches above creak ominously, and the moonlight filters through the twisted canopy in fractured beams, casting strange, shifting patterns on the ground. Shadowy figures flit along the edges of the path, their distorted forms flickering in and out of the mist like phantoms. Their whispers curl through the trees, a mournful murmur that weaves through the leaves like smoke.

"These woods are guarded by spirits who seek to protect the grove," Zephyr says, his luminous gaze fixed ahead. "But the shadows will try to deceive you, twisting your path and clouding your senses."

"How do we navigate the woods?" I ask, glancing nervously at the twisted shapes flickering through the fog. The forest feels like it's breathing, alive with unseen forces.

"Trust in the Luminous Crown," Zephyr replies gently, gesturing toward the circlet cradled in my hands. "Its light will guide you, and the spirits will not oppose those with a pure heart."

I close my eyes, feeling the smooth surface of the circlet beneath my fingers. I begin to murmur an incantation, a spell passed down through generations, taught to me by my grandmother. The words flow from me, imbued with the power to seek guidance and clarity:

"Lumina spiritus, via revelate,

Pura cordis luce, semita illuminate."

The Luminous Crown responds, pulsing with a soft, steady glow that seems to breathe in sync with the incantation. A faint beam of light pierces the mist, cutting a narrow path through the trees. The spectral trail glimmers faintly, beckoning me forward

—a guided pathway only visible to those who invoke the crown's true potential. The connection deepens with each word I speak, intertwining my spirit with the celestial energies of the crown. A surge of confidence fills me; the path it illuminates is true, crafted by my own purity and the ancient wisdom embedded within the Luminous Crown.

"This way," Zephyr calls, his luminous robes trailing through the air as he steps onto the path.

I follow cautiously, my grip tight on the circlet as we tread deeper into the forest. The shadows shift around us, reaching out with twisted fingers that curl through the leaves like tendrils of smoke. Their whispers grow louder, winding through the trees in a mournful hum.

"They will try to sway you from the path," Zephyr warns, glancing back at me over his shoulder. "Focus on the light ahead, and do not heed their voices."

I nod, my breath quickening as the whispers coil around my ears, their words laced with doubt and fear. The path curves sharply, the fog pressing closer, thick and suffocating. The moonlight barely penetrates the twisted canopy, leaving us in a twilight world of shadows and half-seen shapes. My pulse quickens, but I cling to the crown's soft glow, allowing it to steady my nerves as we weave through the shifting darkness.

Finally, the air begins to clear, the oppressive fog lifting as the whispers fade into the night. The path widens before us, the twisted branches parting to reveal a small glade bathed in moonlight. The leaves rustle softly in the breeze, and the air hums with an ancient, powerful energy.

At the center of the glade stands a stone altar, its surface etched with runes that pulse faintly in the silver light. The air ripples with power, and I can feel the warmth of the grove's magick seeping into my chest, infusing me with a sense of belonging and purpose.

"This is the heart of the Wyrd Woods," Zephyr whispers, his gaze fixed on the altar. "The shadows cannot follow you here."

I step forward cautiously, the stone cool beneath my fingertips as I trace the intricate runes carved into its surface. The Luminous Crown hums softly in my hands, and the runes pulse brightly, sending faint tendrils of light curling into the air.

"The magick of the grove resonates within the altar," Zephyr explains, his voice carrying a note of reverence. "Its energy will strengthen your spirit and guide you through the labyrinth."

I close my eyes, feeling the cool, ancient stone beneath my palm. As I press gently against it, I begin to murmur an incantation, drawing on the altar's deep reserves of energy:

"Spiritus silvae, ad me venite,

Per labirynthum, me ducite."

The words, meaning "Spirits of the forest, come to me; through the labyrinth, lead me," resonate with the grove's essence. The altar responds instantly, humming with a vibrant energy that spreads through my body, filling me with renewed strength. The crown in my hands pulses brightly, its light growing stronger with each syllable I speak. The mist around us swirls, seemingly alive, celebrating the ancient bond between the altar and the sacred words. I feel more connected to the grove, my spirit buoyed by its timeless power.

"We must move quickly," Zephyr says softly, his gaze flickering toward the swaying trees. "The shadows are restless, and the grove awaits."

I take a deep breath and nod, turning to Zephyr with renewed determination. "Lead the way."

The mist wraps around us as we leave the glade, but Zephyr's glow cuts through it, guiding me forward with each purposeful step. The shadows whisper along the path, their twisted forms flickering at the edges of my vision, but my spirit remains steady, the grove's magick burning brightly within me. The grove is near, its fire burning brightly in the moonlight, a beacon calling me home.

As the Wyrd Woods slowly recede behind us, the fog begins to thin, revealing the familiar landscape of the sacred grove. Each step carries us closer to the heart of the grove, where the coven awaits, their chanting voices a soft, comforting melody that weaves through the night air. My heart pounds with anticipation as the path curves into a moonlit clearing, revealing the grove in all its ethereal glory.

Towering oaks surround the grove, their ancient branches reaching high into the starry sky, woven together to form a protective canopy. Moonlight streams through the leaves, casting intricate patterns on the forest floor like delicate lace. At the center of the grove stands the sacred fire, its flames flickering warmly in the silver light as the coven gathers around it in a protective circle.

Rowena's platinum curls glow like molten silver in the moonlight, her freckled face radiant as she murmurs calming incantations. Gideon's gray eyes are fixed on the flames, his brow furrowed in concentration as he raises his hands in supplication. Dorian grips his dagger with white-knuckled determination, and Artemis traces protective sigils in the air with sprigs of thyme and lavender woven into her auburn braid.

The others stand alongside them, their voices harmonizing like a haunting melody as they chant together. Thalia, Finnian, Celeste, Ronan, Sylvia, and Basil—all contribute their magickal energy to fortify the circle and strengthen the sacred fire, each incantation woven with love and dedication.

But at the grove's edge, Marina lingers, her hazel eyes narrowed as she watches the coven intently. Her raven-black hair falls in waves around her angular face, and shadows twist at her feet like coiling tendrils, reflecting the darkness she harbors within. Her lips move in a silent incantation, her gaze locked on the sacred fire, its flames wavering in the moonlight as if sensing her presence.

Zephyr steps forward, his luminous robes trailing through the mist as he gestures for me to follow. "The Luminous Crown's light will help you weave the incantation and join your coven. Their voices will guide you."

I step forward, my fingers curled tightly around the smooth circlet as I feel the warmth of the sacred fire on my skin. I close my eyes and begin to murmur an incantation, focusing on the hum of energy that ripples through the air. The Luminous Crown glows brightly in my hands, its light weaving through the mist and spiraling up toward the sacred fire. I channel my intent through the circlet with these words:

"Crown of celestial light, your glow so bright,

Guide my voice through shadowed night.

Let this spell through darkness tear,

Connect my soul to those who care."

As the words leave my lips, the circlet's light intensifies, casting beams that pierce the surrounding gloom, forging a tangible link between me and the distant chants of my coven, their voices echoing back to me through the magickal conduit I've created.

The grove trembles with energy as my voice joins the coven's in harmony, each word a soft hum that vibrates through the air. The flames leap higher, swirling with silver and violet light as they cast long shadows on the forest floor.

Rowena's calming incantations intertwine with mine, her voice ringing out clear and steady as the moonlight pulses through her fingers. She murmurs with soothing clarity:

"Peace be still, calm the storm,

Shield us with the moon's warm,

Serenity bind, fear unwind,

Within these woods, protection find."

Gideon raises his hands, gray eyes glowing with determination as he intones a powerful incantation that strengthens the circle's protective barrier. His voice is firm and commanding as he chants:

"By the force of land and sky,

Circle strong, where no harm nigh,

Guardians call, to this sphere draw,

Bound by light, we stand without flaw."

Dorian and Thalia murmur in unison, their magickal defenses winding through the grove like shimmering threads that weave together in a radiant tapestry. Celeste and Ronan add their voices, creating a melody that hums with the rhythm of ancient magick, the notes intertwining with the very fabric of the night.

But Marina's shadowy tendrils stretch toward the circle, her gaze fixed on the sacred fire as her incantation weaves through the mist. Her lips twist in fury, her voice cold and vengeful as she hisses her dark chant:

"Shadows rise, and flicker flame,

My will be done, my claim to claim,

Fire falter, circle break,

In this night, my power awake."

But the light of the Luminous Crown cuts through the darkness, unraveling her twisted magick strand by strand.

The coven's voices rise, their chanting reaching a crescendo as the circle pulses with radiant energy. The grove glows brightly in the moonlight, the sacred fire burning with silver and violet light that wraps around the grove like a protective veil, countering Marina's dark intentions with the collective power of the coven's unified incantations.

With the final word, "Paciscor,"—conveying the sealing or completion of the spell—the incantation fades, and the grove is filled with peaceful stillness. The flames burn steadily in the moonlight, casting warm shadows on the forest floor, while the circle's protective barrier shimmers softly around the coven, securing their accord with the energies they have summoned.

Marina's shadow retreats, her twisted incantation crumbling beneath the moonlight as the darkness fades into the mist. Her raven-black hair falls across her angular face, and she steps back into the forest with a bitter snarl, her gaze still fixed on the sacred fire.

Rowena reaches out and touches my hand, her freckled face glowing with relief as she smiles warmly. "Soraya, you're back," she whispers, her voice trembling with emotion.

Gideon steps closer, gray eyes brimming with tears as he clasps my hand tightly. "I knew you would return," he murmurs softly, his voice cracking. "Welcome home, High Priestess."

The grove is filled with murmurs of welcome as the coven

surrounds me, their voices harmonizing like a joyful melody as they offer their strength and support. Zephyr's luminous gaze watches from the grove's edge, his robes trailing through the mist as he smiles faintly.

"You have found your way back to the grove," he says softly, his chiming voice echoing through the trees. "The darkness cannot hold you."

I close my eyes, the warmth of the sacred fire filling my spirit as I breathe deeply. "The darkness cannot hold us," I murmur, my voice steady. "Our light will burn brightly in the moonlight."

With the Luminous Crown glowing softly in my hands and the coven gathered around me, I return as High Priestess, the shadows retreating before the radiant light of our magick. Together, we will lift the curse from the grove and protect our circle from the darkness.

CHAPTER 7

THE STAR SEED'S LIGHT

The warmth of the grove wraps around me like a comforting embrace as the coven gathers closer, their voices humming with anticipation. The sacred fire burns brightly in the moonlight, casting shimmering patterns on the forest floor and illuminating the faces of my friends and my family. But the shadows linger at the grove's edge, and Marina's twisted magick still weaves through the mist like a coiling serpent, a reminder of the darkness that seeks to consume us.

Zephyr steps forward, his luminous robes trailing through the mist as he raises his hand toward the sacred fire. "The darkness is weakened but not yet defeated," he intones softly. "To lift the curse and banish the shadows, you must bind Marina's twisted magick and seal the grove in radiant light."

Rowena's freckled face glows with determination as she steps beside me, her platinum curls swaying gently in the moonlight. "Soraya, what do we need to do?"

I clutch the Luminous Crown tightly in my hands, its light

pulsing softly through my fingers. "We must weave an incantation to bind the shadows," I say, my voice steady. "And Marina's magick must be unraveled from within."

Gideon's gray eyes gleam in the firelight as he steps forward, his brow furrowed with concentration. "What will you need?"

"The strength of the coven," I reply, turning to face the circle. "We must channel our energy through the Luminous Crown and weave our voices together to bind the shadows."

Artemis nods, her green eyes shining with resolve. "We'll stand with you."

Thalia hums a soft tune under her breath, her robes swirling around her as she smiles confidently. "Let's show these shadows what we're made of."

I step forward, the Luminous Crown glowing brightly in my grasp. "Friends, this is Zephyr," I begin, my voice carrying across the grove. "He has guided me through the labyrinth, helping me to uncover the depths of Marina's deceit. He brings with him the wisdom of the ancients, insights that have long been hidden from us."

Zephyr nods respectfully to the coven. "Greetings," he says, his voice calm and soothing. "Soraya is right. Marina has woven a tapestry of shadows that threaten to engulf all that is light within this grove. Together, we have the power to untangle this dark weave."

Rowena steps closer, her curiosity piqued. "How did Marina come to betray us?" she asks, her voice a whisper in the quiet night.

I pause, feeling the weight of my lineage pressing against my chest, the truth that I've only recently uncovered beginning to take form in my mind. "It began long ago," I say, my voice deepening with the gravity of our history. "During the witch trials, Marina's ancestor deceived my great-great-grandmother, a betrayal that set a curse into motion, a dark shadow that has lingered and grown through the generations."

Zephyr's gaze meets each of us as he explains further, "Marina has been seduced by the promise of power beyond her reach, a power that corrupts without the balance of the light we cherish. Her heart has darkened, and she seeks to dominate the grove's magick for her own gain, just as her ancestor once did."

Artemis frowns, her hands tightening into fists. "What must we do to stop her?"

"We need to act swiftly," I say, feeling the weight of our task. "Zephyr and I have prepared a binding spell that will strip away the shadows Marina has called forth. But we need your help to amplify its strength."

The coven members nod, their faces set with determination. Gideon steps forward, his voice steady, "Tell us what to do. We stand ready."

Zephyr and I exchange a glance, and then I take a deep breath, feeling the power of the cosmos coursing through my veins—a reminder of my heritage, a connection to the stars that has always been a part of me.

There's a moment of silence as I prepare to speak, a pause that seems to stretch beyond the confines of the grove, reaching into the distant stars where my lineage began. The realization hits me fully now: I am a Star seed, a being whose spirit was born in the heart of a distant constellation, sent to Earth with a purpose that I'm only beginning to understand.

"Before we begin," I say, my voice carrying the weight of this newfound knowledge, "there's something I need to share with you all. My connection to the Luminous Crown isn't just because of my training or our shared history. It's because I'm a Star seed. But more than that, all of us here are Star seeds."

The grove falls silent, the crackling of the fire the only sound as my words sink in. Rowena's eyes widen, and she steps closer, her voice barely a whisper. "A Star seed… you mean our spirits come from the stars?"

I nod, feeling a deep sense of peace wash over me as I speak the truth. "Yes. Our spirits were born in various constellations across the galaxy, each of us carrying the wisdom and energy of different star systems. Some of you may have felt this connection, a pull toward something greater, but you haven't fully understood it until now. We don't all come from the same star system—I, for instance, am from the Orion constellation—but some of you may hail from different origins. The Pleiades, Andromeda, Sirius… we are all connected to the cosmos in our own unique ways."

Gideon looks at me with awe in his eyes, his voice hushed. "That's why you've always felt so… otherworldly, so connected to something beyond this realm."

I smile, the warmth of their acceptance filling me with renewed strength. "Exactly. And now, it's time for all of us to awaken to our true nature. The power of the stars isn't just within me—it's within all of you as well. We each bring something unique from our star origins. Together, we'll use that connection to banish the shadows and restore the light to our grove."

Zephyr nods, his eyes shining with pride. "Your lineage is your strength, Soraya. And so is the lineage of every person here.

With the power of the stars within you, we can undo the darkness that Marina has wrought."

With the coven gathered close, I begin to chant, my voice rising with the power of our united front. The coven joins in, their voices melding into a powerful chorus that fills the grove with vibrating energy, the very air humming with the resonance of our combined magick.

As we chant, the crown in my hands pulsates with a fierce light, and the shadows at the edges of the grove begin to falter and withdraw. Marina, hidden within the mist, lets out a cry of rage as her dark magick begins to unravel, the power of the stars overwhelming her shadowy tendrils.

The fire crackles and hisses, its flames dancing wildly as our voices rise. "We bind you, Marina, and your shadows," we declare, our words a powerful spell of containment and protection, infused with the energy of the stars that birthed our spirits.

The grove trembles under the force of our magick, the sacred fire glowing brighter than ever before. As the final echo of our chant dies away, a deep, resonant peace settles over the grove. Marina's presence recedes, her power waning under the strength of our collective will, amplified by the starbound energy that flows through each of us.

"We have done it," I say, the relief evident in my voice as I look around at the circle of my coven. "The grove is safe once more, thanks to each of you, and Zephyr's guidance."

Zephyr nods, his eyes bright with unspoken pride. "Your unity is your strength. And your heritage, Soraya, is your greatest gift. Remember this night, the night you reclaimed your power and protected your sacred space. And remember, this power belongs to all of you."

The coven murmurs in agreement, their faces reflecting the firelight, strong and serene. As we disperse, the feeling of victory and the warmth of the grove envelop us, a reminder that together, we are indeed powerful beyond measure.

As I stand by the sacred fire, feeling the gentle pulse of the Luminous Crown in my hands, I know that this is only the beginning. My journey as a Star seed is just unfolding, and with my coven by my side, I will help each of them awaken to their own celestial origins. Together, there's no limit to the light we can bring to this world.

Chapter 8

The Labyrinth's Test

In the luminous embrace of the sacred fire, the grove hums with a rejuvenated peace, as if the very air is alive with a newfound harmony. The Luminous Crown pulses gently in my hands, sending tendrils of light weaving through our protective circle, stitching the air with shimmering threads of energy. Around me, the coven murmurs in relieved whispers, their faces reflecting the warm glow of the fire as the shadows that once threatened us dissolve into the encroaching mist.

Despite the calm, Zephyr's gaze remains vigilant, fixed on the edges of the grove where the darkness lingers like a stubborn stain. His robes, pale as moonlight, flutter softly in the breeze, creating an ethereal aura around him. He steps forward, his voice chiming melodically, carrying a hint of urgency. "The veil may be unraveling, but remnants of Marina's twisted magick still linger beyond our sanctuary."

Gideon, his gray eyes determined, meets my gaze with a steady resolve. "What's our next move?"

I study the Luminous Crown, its warm glow casting playful shadows across the forest floor, a reminder of the light we've fought to preserve. "We need to purge the remnants of her curse from the labyrinth itself. Only by lifting her residual influence can we secure the grove's safety."

Rowena, her curls kissed by moonlight, nods with resolve, her freckled face glowing with determination. "How can we assist?"

"We must split our efforts," Zephyr suggests, his luminous eyes scanning our group with a calm yet focused intensity. "Each team will tackle a different segment of the labyrinth, unraveling Marina's dark webs to weaken her grip."

Artemis steps up, her gaze unwavering, her voice steady. "Guide us."

Clutching the Luminous Crown tighter, feeling its light throb in sync with my heartbeat, I direct them. "Gideon, Rowena, and Artemis, head north through the Wyrd Woods. Basil and Dorian, take your group to the Abyssal Chasm to clear any shadows Marina left behind."

Thalia's eyes sparkle like the stars above, her usual lighthearted demeanor giving way to serious intent. "And my group?"

"You, Thalia, along with Finnian, Celeste, Ronan, and Sylvia, will join me and Zephyr to fortify the Moonlit Labyrinth," I say, catching Zephyr's affirming nod. "We'll cast a protective spell to prevent Marina's darkness from seeping back in."

With understanding nods, the coven divides, their footsteps soft against the earth as they set out on their designated paths. Zephyr and I lead our group, the Luminous Crown guiding us with its radiant glow, cutting through the fog that clings to the twisted oak trees and winding paths at the labyrinth's edge.

As we venture deeper, the atmosphere thickens, the air charged with a sense of anticipation. Thalia begins to hum, her voice a melodious beacon in the damp air, a thread of hope weaving through the tension. Beside us, Finnian, now in the form of a sleek fox, moves with silent grace, his keen senses alert to any disturbance. Celeste's lips move in silent communion with the astral plane, her focus is unwavering, while Ronan's hands dance through the air, crafting spells that weave around us like protective silk. Sylvia's quiet chants ripple softly, mingling with the shadows and turning them away, her magick a soothing balm against the darkness.

Zephyr, ever graceful, leads with a steadiness that reassures me, his presence a calming anchor in the swirling uncertainty. "The Moonlit Labyrinth mirrors your deepest memories and fears, Soraya. Marina's curse has twisted these paths into knots of dark energy. We must unravel her influence here."

Lifting the Luminous Crown, I let its light scatter high above us, casting silver beams that slice through the mist like a sword cutting through the gloom. "Gather close," I whisper, my breath visible in the cool air. "We need to unify our voices for the incantation."

Forming a circle, the grove a faint glow in the distance, we each raise our hands. Zephyr, at the center, fixes his gaze on the pulsating crown, his expression one of intense focus. I close my eyes, take a deep breath, and start to murmur the words of old, feeling the crown respond with surges of energy, a connection deepening between us and the stars.

"In the name of Orion, where our journey begins,
    By the light of Eridanus, our ancient kin,
    With the power of Lyra, we summon the stars,
    From the Pleiades, our strength transcends the scars,
    Sirius shines, with wisdom so bright,
    And from Andromeda, we draw endless light.
    Together we stand, bound by fate,
    As one, we rise, to seal Marina's gate."

Thalia's voice intertwines with mine, lifting the melody into the night, a song that speaks of unity and strength. Ronan and Sylvia join in, their voices adding layers of power and depth, creating a resonance that fills the labyrinth with light. Finnian circles us, his animal instincts on high alert, guarding our sacred task with a watchful eye.

The Luminous Crown vibrates intensely, waves of light rippling outward, illuminating the labyrinth's convoluted paths. The shadows twist and recoil under our combined power, their essence crumbling as our spell permeates the air, dissolving the knots of dark energy Marina had woven into the fabric of this place.

The labyrinth reacts; paths that were once twisted now straighten, the deceitful turns and dead ends imposed by Marina's will begin to dissolve. Her lingering darkness fades, the malicious whispers dying away under the relentless assault of our light, a light born of our unity and my Star Seed heritage.

As our incantation reaches its crescendo, the air stills, and the labyrinth settles into a new, untainted alignment. The Luminous Crown's glow softens, bathing us in gentle light as the pathways clear, the last remnants of Marina's influence dissipating into the night.

Zephyr, his robes barely stirring in the now calm air, steps closer to inspect the crown. "The veil thins," he murmurs, his voice thoughtful, "but shadows still cling to the periphery."

I nod, my resolve hardening into something unbreakable. "Then we continue. We cleanse the labyrinth until a trace of darkness does not remain."

With renewed purpose, we retrace our steps through the labyrinth, guided by the crown's unwavering light. The sacred fire in the distance remains a bright beacon, its flames a testament to our progress and a signal of hope that burns brightly in the heart of the grove.

As we move forward, the first group appears from the northern path through the Wyrd Woods. Gideon, Rowena, and Artemis emerge, their faces reflecting a mixture of relief and resolve. Rowena's hand rests lightly on Artemis's shoulder, a gesture of quiet reassurance, while Gideon strides confidently beside them, his gaze meeting mine with a look that says their mission was successful.

Further along the path, Basil and Dorian step out from the shadows of the Abyssal Chasm. Basil adjusts his glasses, his calm demeanor masking the intensity of what they've just faced. Dorian walks beside him, ever vigilant, his eyes scanning the area to ensure we are all safe as we converge. The two of them exchange a glance, a silent confirmation that the shadows Marina left behind have been cleared.

From the depths of the labyrinth, our final group emerges. Thalia leads the way, her eyes sparkling with a triumphant light. Behind her, Finnian moves with his usual grace, his senses heightened, ensuring no danger lurks nearby. Celeste, with her dreamy expression, walks alongside Ronan, who carries an air of quiet confidence. Sylvia brings up the rear, her presence ghostly yet grounding, a reminder of the delicate balance we maintain between light and dark.

Zephyr, ever the guide, falls into step beside me, their luminous eyes reflecting the glow of the Luminous Crown still pulsating in my hands. Together, we lead the group back to the grove, where the sacred fire burns bright, welcoming us all home.

As we emerge from the labyrinth, the sense of accomplishment is palpable, a quiet victory that resonates in our shared silence. The grove stands before us, the sacred fire burning bright, welcoming us back as one. With Marina's influence waning, the path forward is clearer, but I know that the complete lifting of the veil requires more—five precise steps to banish the darkness entirely, steps that I feel instinctively drawn to complete.

Standing by the fire, its warmth seeping into my bones and chasing away the last remnants of cold, I feel a mix of exhaustion and exhilaration. Tonight, we have turned the tide, a crucial victory in our ongoing battle against the shadows. The fire crackles, a lively dance of sparks that seem to celebrate our triumph, a beacon that promises to guide us through whatever darkness lies ahead.

Zephyr stands beside me, his luminous presence a steady comfort. "You've done well, Soraya. Your connection to the stars is your greatest strength, but it's your connection to your coven that has brought you here."

I smile, feeling the truth of his words settle in my heart.

"Together, we're stronger than any darkness. And with the stars to guide us, there's nothing we can't overcome."

The grove is quiet now, the shadows gone, replaced by a serene peace that fills the air. The coven gathers around the fire, their faces lit by its warm glow, their expressions a mix of relief and determination. We have won a battle, but the war is not yet over.

As I look around at the faces of my friends and my family, I know that whatever comes next, we will face it together. The light of the Luminous Crown pulses softly in my hands, a reminder of the power we wield, not just as witches, but as beings connected to something greater, something infinite.

Tonight, we have banished the darkness from the labyrinth, but I feel a new journey calling me, one that will take me even deeper into the mysteries of my Star seed lineage and the ancient magick that flows through my veins. With my coven by my side, and the light of the stars to guide us, I am ready for whatever lies ahead.

CHAPTER 9

THE FINAL BINDING

As the moon climbs high, its beams lay a silvery sheen over the grove, bathing the faces of my coven in ethereal light. We gather together, our spirits lifted, buoyed by the victories we've shared tonight. The Luminous Crown in my hands pulses with a serene, confident glow, its light casting gentle shadows that dance across the forest floor. The expressions on my friends' and family's faces reflect a mix of relief and resolve, the weight of what we've achieved settling into our bones.

We form a circle, and Zephyr steps into the center, his presence as calm and steady as the cool night breeze. His luminous robes flutter softly, catching the moonlight as he addresses us with a solemn nod. "The shadows have indeed receded, and our paths are now clear, yet we stand at the threshold of a crucial act—one that will ensure our grove's protection for all time," he declares, his voice carrying the weight of history and hope, resonating through the still air.

Rowena steps forward, her curls catching the moonlight like

threads of silver. Her eyes meet mine, sparking with unyielding determination. "Let's bind Marina's lingering magick with a seal that only the true heart of

this coven can ever unlock," she suggests, her voice fierce and sure.

I nod, feeling the familiar weight of my responsibilities as High Priestess settle on my shoulders. "Yes, let's weave the Final Binding," I propose, lifting the Luminous Crown high. Its light flares in response, casting a warm glow over the circle. "This act will safeguard our sacred grounds from the taint of darkness forevermore."

Gideon steps beside me, his steady presence a reassuring force. Together, we begin to guide the coven in a powerful incantation, invoking the ancient forces that have watched over our lands for centuries. The sacred fire before us crackles and roars to life, as if feeding off our collective energy, its flames dancing higher as our voices rise in unison:

"Guardians of the grove, hear our plea,

Bind the darkness, set us free.

With heart and spirit, we call to thee,

Seal this ground from bane and glee."

Around us, Thalia and Sylvia weave their voices into a harmonious tapestry, their incantations reinforcing the growing barrier around us:

"Elements of earth and air,

Consecrate this sacred lair.

Water, fire, heed our call,

Protect this grove, stand tall and gall."

Ronan, ever the skilled technomancer, casts spells that draw glowing, intricate patterns in the night air, each symbol sealing the magick within our circle. His chant melds technology with ancient words, his voice steady and rhythmic:

"Circuits of old and new, intertwine,

Magick bound, by design.

Shield and cloak, ward and bind,

In this circle, safety find."

Artemis and Dorian maintain a vigilant watch, their eyes scanning the perimeters of our sacred space, ensuring that no trace of Marina's corruption lingers in the land. Their words are a quiet but firm guard against any remaining dark tendrils:

"From shadow's grip, we claim release,

From outer dark, bring inner peace.

Let no malice pass our ward,

In this grove, let discord be barred."

As our ritual crescendos, the Luminous Crown bursts forth with blinding light, its energy sweeping through the grove like a purifying tidal wave. The lingering shadows recoil, their final whispers of resistance fading into nothingness as the crown's light binds them at the forest's edge.

With the completion of the Final Binding, our grove is not just secured—it is sanctified, its magick sealed by the unity and strength of our coven. Marina's corruptive influence is obliterated, leaving behind nothing but the echoes of her betrayal.

We then gather around the sacred fire, the warmth of our bond palpable in the air. The grove, now vibrant with tranquility and power, hums with the collective strength of our spirits, a living testament to our resilience and dedication.

Zephyr, looking around at the illuminated faces, his eyes reflecting the fire's warm glow, smiles broadly. "Tonight, you have achieved more than just the protection of this grove; you have reclaimed its sanctity," he praises, his voice imbued with pride and warmth.

Gideon stands close to me, his gray eyes soft with relief and admiration. "We did it, Soraya," he murmurs, his voice low and filled with emotion. "The grove is safe, and so are we."

I nod, the weight of the night's events finally easing off my shoulders. "Yes, we did," I reply, a smile tugging at the corners of my lips. "But it was all of us—together."

Rowena laughs softly, the sound like the tinkling of wind chimes. "I'm just glad we don't have to deal with any more of Marina's shadowy nonsense," she says, her tone light but her eyes serious.

Thalia grins, her eyes twinkling with mischief. "I'd say we showed those shadows what we're made of, don't you think?"

"Absolutely," Artemis agrees, a smile breaking through her usual stoic expression. "We've strengthened our bond and our grove."

The night unfolds in a celebration that fills the grove with music and laughter, the light from the fire dancing in our eyes. We revel not just as survivors of darkness but as its conquerors— as the keepers of the light. The grove, our sanctuary, stands stronger than ever, a beacon of hope and magick beneath the celestial gaze of the stars.

As dawn's light begins to streak the sky, signaling the approach of a new day, we stand together, united. The grove is quiet now, the shadows gone, replaced by a serene peace that fills the air. The coven gathers close, the bonds between us stronger than ever.

Zephyr's voice breaks the comfortable silence. "You've done

more than protect the grove tonight," he says, his tone filled with pride. "You've proven the strength of your unity, the power of your light. Whatever darkness may come, you will face it together, and you will prevail."

I look around at the faces of my friends and my family, feel a deep sense of contentment settle in my heart. The Luminous Crown pulses softly in my hands; its light is a reminder of the power we wield, not just as witches but as beings connected to something greater, something infinite.

Tonight, we have banished the darkness from the labyrinth, but I know this is only the beginning. My journey as a Star seed, as the High Priestess of this coven, is just unfolding. With my coven by my side, and the light of the stars to guide us, we are ready for whatever lies ahead.

As the first rays of dawn break through the canopy, casting golden light over the grove, we stand together, stronger than ever. Our hearts and spirits are forever intertwined with the fate of the grove, and under the watchful eyes of the stars and the gentle caress of the dawn, we are reminded of the enduring power of unity and the relentless strength of light over darkness.

But even as the morning light begins to paint the horizon in shades of rose and gold, I feel a new journey calling me—one that will take me deeper into the mysteries of my Star seed lineage. The ancient magick that flows through my veins has only begun to reveal its true nature. There are secrets hidden within the stars, secrets that call to me now more than ever. The Luminous Crown pulses in my hands, as if in agreement, its light promising guidance as I prepare to embark on this new path. My coven will be by my side, their strength and love a constant source of power as we venture into the unknown.

And so, with the dawn of a new day, we stand on the precipice of an even greater journey, one that will test our bonds, challenge our understanding of magick, and reveal the true extent of our power. The light of the stars shines brightly above us, a beacon guiding us forward, reminding us that no matter how deep the darkness, the light will always find a way to shine through.

CHAPTER 10

THE STAR SEED AWAKENING

As dawn breaks, the first golden rays of sunlight filter through the ancient trees, casting a warm, ethereal glow across the grove. The sacred fire, once roaring, has settled into a gentle flicker, its embers glowing softly as they reflect the calm that has finally descended upon us. The air is filled with a serene stillness, broken only by the quiet rustle of leaves and the faint, lingering scent of last night's powerful magick. We gather in a close circle, our hearts still beating with the shared triumph of our victory.

Gideon stands beside me, his hand warm and reassuring in mine. His gray eyes, softened by the early morning light, are filled with a quiet strength and understanding. "The grove feels different now," he says, his voice low and contemplative. "It's as if it's breathing with new life, connected to us in a way it never was before."

I nod, sensing the same shift. There's an undeniable connection between us and the land, a pulse of energy that seems to flow from the earth itself, threading through each of us like a living current. "We've done more than just reclaim the grove," I say softly, my gaze sweeping over the familiar faces of my coven. "When Zephyr led me to the Celestial Tower, we uncovered something extraordinary—a hidden chamber beneath our altar. That's where we discovered the Celestial Circle, the source of the grove's power."

Zephyr, ever the wise guide, steps forward, his robes catching the soft light of dawn. "You've touched on something deeper, Soraya," he says, his voice resonating with the truth of ages. "The shadows may have been driven back, but in their wake, they've revealed a hidden truth. The Star Seed lineage isn't just within you—it's within all of us. It's the ancient magick that connects every living being to the cosmos, a thread of light that we all carry within. The Celestial Circle you discovered is the focal point of that connection, the heart of this grove's power."

Rowena, her curls glowing like threads of spun silver, looks at me with wide eyes, realization dawning on her face. "You mean... we're all connected to this ancient power? Not just those of us with a direct lineage, but everyone?"

Zephyr nods, his gaze steady and knowing. "Yes, Rowena. The Star Seed lineage is the birthright of every soul on this earth. It's the cosmic connection that binds us to the universe, to each other, and to the very magick that flows through our veins. Last night's victory wasn't just about protecting the grove—it was about awakening to this truth, and the Celestial Circle is the key to unlocking that power."

Thalia steps closer, her eyes bright with wonder and curiosity. "So, you're saying that this power, this ancient magick, is something we can all tap into? That it's not just a matter of bloodlines or heritage?"

"Yes," I reply, feeling the truth of it settle deep within my bones. "We've all felt it, haven't we? That pull, that connection to something greater than us. It's the Star Seed within us—the light of the stars that guides us, that flows through us, and that connects us to the universe and each other. And now that we've found the Celestial Circle, we can fully harness that connection."

Gideon squeezes my hand, his expression one of deep thought. "It makes sense. The way we've been able to stand against the darkness, the way our voices and magick have harmonized—it's not just skill or training. It's this connection, this Star Seed magick, that's empowered us, and the Celestial Circle is amplifying that power."

Zephyr's voice is filled with quiet pride as he continues, "And it's this realization that will guide you on your next journey. The path ahead isn't just about uncovering ancient secrets or mastering new spells—it's about embracing this connection and understanding that the power within each of you is part of something much larger. The stars themselves have always been a part of you, and now that you've awakened to this truth, your potential is limitless."

Artemis, always the protector, steps forward with a new resolve in her eyes. "This changes everything. If we're all connected to the Star Seed, then our strength isn't just in our individual abilities—it's in our unity, our collective will, especially now that we know the Celestial Circle is there to anchor us."

I smile, feeling a deep sense of peace settle over me. "Exactly, Artemis. The Star Seed within us is a reminder that we are never alone. We are all part of this vast, cosmic web, and together, we can achieve anything. The challenges we've faced have shown us that, but the journey ahead will take us even deeper into this understanding."

Rowena's eyes shine with a renewed sense of purpose. "We've always been stronger together, but now we know why. This isn't just about us—it's about every living being, every soul that carries the light of the stars within them."

Thalia grins, her playful spirit undimmed by the weight of our revelation. "I've always known we were special, but this? This is on a whole new level. We've got the universe on our side!"

The grove seems to hum with approval, the energy of our collective realization feeding back into the earth, the trees, the very air around us. The Luminous Crown pulses once more in my hands, its light growing brighter as if acknowledging our shared understanding.

As the sun climbs higher in the sky, casting a golden light over the grove, I know that the journey ahead will be one of discovery—of who we are, of the ancient magick that flows through us, and of the vast, cosmic connection that binds us all together. The labyrinth was just the beginning. Now, with our eyes opened to the truth of our Star Seed lineage, we are ready to explore the mysteries that await us.

Together, we step forward into the dawn of a new adventure, guided by the light of the stars and the knowledge that we are all part of something infinitely greater. Whatever challenges lie ahead, we will face them as one—united, empowered, and connected to the very heart of the universe.

Chapter 11

Echoes of the Ancestors

The afternoon sun filters through the ancient oak trees, casting a warm, golden light that dapples the earth beneath our feet. The grove hums with a quiet energy, a subtle yet potent reminder of the power that flows through this sacred place. The air is thick with the scent of earth and leaves, mingling with the faint aroma of incense that still lingers from our earlier rituals. This grove, our sanctuary, has weathered countless storms, but the peace we feel now is hard-won and deeply cherished.

We stand together beneath the sprawling branches of the oldest oak—a tree that has borne silent witness to centuries of our lineage. It is here, under this canopy of ancient wisdom, that Zephyr calls us to action. His voice is soft yet carries the weight of countless generations, resonating through the grove like a whisper from the past. "The shadows cast by Marina's magick run deep," he begins, his eyes scanning the faces of the coven, "but they are not permanent scars. Today, we must call upon our ancestors, drawing on their wisdom and strength, to cleanse these remnants once and for all."

As Zephyr speaks, I step into the center of our circle, holding the Luminous Crown, its soft, pulsing light a beacon of hope. The crown seems to respond to the gravity of the moment, its glow intensifying as if acknowledging the task ahead. I meet the eyes of my fellow coven members, drawing strength from their unwavering resolve. "To invoke the spirits of our ancestors and harness their power," I say, my voice clear and strong, "we must perform the Ancestral Summoning Incantation. This rite will bridge our world with theirs, allowing their ancient energies to aid us in our quest."

A deep silence falls over the grove, the air thick with anticipation. Together, we raise our voices, the words of the incantation blending into a chorus that resonates with the very heart of the grove:

"Præteriti spiritus, ad nos huc venite, catenas frangite!"

(Spirits of the past, come to us here, break the chains!)

As our voices rise, the air around us begins to shimmer, the boundary between realms growing thin. Ethereal figures materialize at the edges of the grove, their forms wavering like mirages before solidifying into clear, distinct shapes. The ancestral spirits—majestic and mysterious—move among us, their eyes glowing with the wisdom of ages.

Rowena and Artemis, their purpose united, begin their Protective Weaving Incantation. Their hands move in graceful arcs, tracing ancient symbols in the air as they chant:

"Protegamus et custodiamus, semitas nostras claras servemus!"

(Let us protect and guard, keep our paths clear!)

Their voices intertwine, creating a luminous shield that encircles the grove. The shield is a shimmering web of pure magick, its light pulsating with energy, reinforcing the barrier that protects our sacred space from any lingering darkness.

Dorian, his gaze intense and focused, begins his Path Clearing Chant, his deep voice resonating with authority as he works to purify the labyrinth's twisted pathways, tainted by Marina's dark magick:

"Expurgate tenebras, renovate lucem!"

(Expel the darkness, renew the light!)

A wave of light travels along the labyrinth's corridors, burning away the shadows and leaving behind a trail of peace. The once menacing twists and turns of the labyrinth now glow with a soft, welcoming light, transformed from a place of fear into one of serenity.

Beside me, Gideon, his expression solemn and determined, starts his Incantation for Unraveling, his voice steady as he works to dissolve the harmful bindings left by Marina's spells:

"Solvite nociva, ligamina soluta!"

(Dissolve the harmful, let bindings be undone!)

His words cut through the air like a blade, unraveling the remnants of dark magick until they dissolve into nothingness. The atmosphere lightens as the last traces of Marina's influence are stripped away, leaving the grove purified and renewed.

As our chants intertwine, the ancestral spirits nod in approval, their ethereal forms glowing with a celestial light. They move among us, touching our shoulders; whispering words of encouragement and strength. Their presence amplifies our magick, making it stronger, more potent, and deeply connected to the earth beneath our feet.

The grove thrums with power, alive with the energies of centuries of guardianship. As the ancestral spirits begin to fade, their mission complete, they leave behind a profound sense of empowerment and unity among us. The connection to our lineage feels both purified and strengthened, as if the very roots of the grove have been invigorated by their touch.

As the sun dips lower in the sky, casting long shadows across the grove, we gather around the sacred fire, now blazing with a bright, clear flame that reflects the purity of our intentions. The fire crackles warmly, its light dancing in our eyes as we share stories of our ancestors, recounting tales of ancient magick and celebrated triumphs. Each story knits us closer together, and the bond between us is as strong as the magick that flows through the grove.

Rowena's voice rises above the crackle of the fire, her tone filled with reverence as she speaks of her great-grandmother, a powerful witch who once protected the grove from invaders. Artemis follows, her voice steady as she recounts the story of her ancestor who mastered the art of scrying, foreseeing dangers that threatened our sanctuary.

Gideon, his voice rich and warm, tells of his ancestor, a man known for his unshakable courage, who led the coven through one of its darkest times. His words resonate with pride, and I can see in his eyes the same determination that must have burned in his ancestor's heart.

When it's my turn, I speak of the Star seeds, of the celestial lineage that I've recently come to understand. I tell them of the distant stars where our spirits were born, of the cosmic energies that flow through us, connecting us to something greater, something infinite. The coven listens in silence, their faces reflecting the same awe and wonder that I feel.

As the stories wind down and the fire burns lower, we sit in a comfortable silence, the air around us thick with the presence of our ancestors. I feel their strength within me, a warmth that fills my chest and spreads through my limbs, grounding me in the knowledge that I am part of something vast and enduring.

The sun finally sets, casting the grove into twilight. The stars begin to emerge, one by one, their light twinkling through the canopy above. We stand together, our hearts and spirits intertwined, ready to face whatever challenges may come, knowing that we are backed by the power of our ancestors and the unbreakable bonds of our community.

As the last embers of the fire die out, we rise, our movements slow and deliberate, as if savoring the moment. The grove is quiet, the air cool and still, but there is a sense of peace that wasn't there before. We have done what needed to be done, and in doing so, we have strengthened not just our sanctuary, but ourselves.

Hand in hand, we leave the grove, the echoes of our ancestors' voices still lingering in our ears, a reminder that we are never alone. We are the guardians of this sacred place, and with the power of the past behind us, we will continue to protect it, ensuring that its light never fades.

CHAPTER 12

THE UNVEILING OF THE STAR SEED PATH

The lingering essence of the ancestral spirits still perfumes the air, their presence a subtle yet powerful reminder of the strength that courses through our lineage. As the shadows that Marina cast over our sacred grove begin to dissipate, a newfound clarity washes over us. Yet, even as the surface brightens, the remnants of her dark magick cling stubbornly to the deepest recesses of the labyrinth, their insidious presence a testament to the challenge that still lies ahead. Our journey is far from over, and the path before us remains shrouded in mystery, danger lurking within every twist and turn.

Tonight, we gather again in the grove, the weight of the previous night's revelations still fresh in our minds. Night has fully claimed the grove, its darkness thick and impenetrable, save for the sacred fire burning defiantly at the center of our circle. The flames flicker and dance, casting long, wavering shadows that ripple across our faces, reflecting the tension and resolve that grips each of us. The air is heavy with anticipation;

every breath drawn in the silence feels as though it might tip the balance between triumph and disaster.

I stand beside the fire, the Luminous Crown cradled in my hands, its warmth seeping into my skin, a steady pulse that matches the rhythm of my heartbeat. The light within the crown glows softly, a beacon of hope and strength, a reminder of the power we hold as a united coven. "The path ahead is fraught with peril," I announce, my voice cutting through the crisp night air with the weight of our task. The words linger in the stillness, hanging heavy with the gravity of what is to come. "Marina's core enchantments lie deep within the labyrinth, shielded by her most potent spells. To break them, we must be both strong and cunning, relying on our bond and our shared purpose."

Zephyr steps forward, his eyes catching the fire's glow, his robes whispering against the night breeze as he moves. "We will divide into three groups to navigate this final stretch," he explains, his tone calm but laced with urgency. "Each group will dismantle a specific aspect of Marina's remaining magick. Remember, the success of one group depends on the success of the others. The enchantments are interconnected, forming a complex web of dark energy."

Gideon and Artemis take charge of the first group. Their mission is to confront and dispel the illusions that distort reality within the labyrinth. These are no mere tricks of the light; they are deep, psychological traps meant to unhinge us and keep us from our goal. Only by seeing through them can we hope to move forward. Gideon's steadfast nature, combined with Artemis's keen understanding of illusion magick, makes them the ideal pair for this challenge. They exchange a brief look of mutual trust and determination before setting off, their figures quickly swallowed by the shadows of the labyrinth.

Rowena and Dorian are tasked with leading the second group. Their goal is to breach the enchanted barriers guarding the labyrinth's core. These barriers are not merely physical obstacles; they are layered with complex wards and counter-spells designed to repel any who attempt to breach them. Rowena's expertise in dismantling such barriers, paired with Dorian's strategic mind and physical strength, are crucial to their success. As they disappear into the darkness, I whisper a silent prayer for their safety, knowing the magnitude of the task they face.

I will lead the third group, along with Thalia and Ronan. Our task is the most formidable: to confront, unravel, and neutralize the epicenter of Marina's power. This will require not only immense magical strength but also deep personal resolve. The core of Marina's dark magick is a place where her will is strongest, and it will take everything we have to defeat it. Thalia and Ronan stand by my side, their expressions mirroring the determination and courage I feel within myself. With a nod of mutual understanding, we step forward into the labyrinth's depths.

The labyrinth seems almost alive, reacting to our presence with a malevolent awareness. The air grows thicker and more oppressive, and the shadows twist and curl around the winding paths as if the very forest is conspiring against us. The nearly full moon casts a silvery light that struggles to penetrate the dense canopy, giving the forest an eerie, otherworldly glow. Every step feels heavy, laden with the anticipation of what lies ahead, the ground beneath our feet seeming to shift and change with each passing moment.

Guided by the glow of our enchanted artifacts and fueled by our collective will, each group delves deeper into the labyrinth. We encounter a gauntlet of mystical traps, spectral guardians, and enigmatic puzzles designed to test not just our magick but our very resolve. The path is treacherous, and at times, it feels as though the labyrinth itself is fighting against us, determined to protect the dark secrets it holds.

Zephyr remains in the grove, his chants weaving through the air, creating a protective aura that bolsters us as we navigate the labyrinth. His powerful incantations maintain a lifeline of energy that keeps us connected to the grove, a protective embrace that extends beyond the physical boundaries of our sanctuary. His voice, carried on the wind, is a constant reminder of the strength and support that lie behind us, pushing us forward and urging us to succeed.

As I move deeper into the labyrinth, I begin to see things that I shouldn't be able to—glimpses of what my coven members are enduring in their own battles. It's as if a veil has lifted, granting me a special sight, a connection to them that transcends the physical. Perhaps it's the power of the Celestial Circle coursing through me, or maybe the labyrinth itself is revealing these visions, but I can see it all.

Gideon and Artemis find themselves battling illusions that prey on their deepest fears. I watch, heart pounding, as these apparitions—dark, twisted reflections of their innermost anxieties—manifest around them. These aren't just figments of their imagination; they are manifestations of the labyrinth's dark will, designed to unnerve and disorient. But even through the layers of deception, I can see Gideon's steady presence anchoring them, and Artemis's sharp mind slicing through the illusions, revealing the truth hidden beneath the veils of darkness.

Meanwhile, I catch sight of Rowena and Dorian as they navigate a labyrinth of arcane locks and wards, each more intricate and dangerous than the last. The barriers seem insurmountable, designed to repel any who attempt to breach them, but Rowena's skill in counter-magick and Dorian's methodical approach slowly unravel these defenses. Every lock that clicks open, every ward that fizzles out under their touch, feels like a triumph that I can almost touch myself, bringing us all one step closer to our goal.

This sight—this connection to my coven—drives me forward, fueling my determination. We are not just individuals fighting separate battles; we are a united force, linked by our shared struggles and victories, each of us playing a crucial role in unraveling the labyrinth's dark secrets.

In the labyrinth's heart, Thalia, Ronan, and I finally reach the nexus of Marina's dark magick. The power here is almost tangible, a thick, pulsating energy that hums with malevolence, seeping into the very stones of the labyrinth, making the air around us feel heavy and oppressive, pressing down on us like a physical weight. The darkness is so thick it feels as though it could swallow us whole.

I raise the Luminous Crown, its light flaring brightly, casting long beams that pierce the encroaching darkness. The surge of power that courses through me is unlike anything I've felt before. It's as if the very stars themselves are lending their light to our cause, their ancient energy flowing through my veins. I can feel the connection to my Star Seed lineage deepening, the celestial origins of my spirit awakening fully in this moment.

"This is the moment," I declare, my voice ringing with authority and conviction, cutting through the darkness like a blade. "Here, we end Marina's dominion over our sacred grove. Together, we reclaim our destiny."

Our voices rise as one, a symphony of incantations that spirals into the darkness, weaving a complex tapestry of light and sound. The labyrinth trembles in response, the air saturated with the energy of creation and destruction, resonating with the finality of our resolve. The power of our combined magick flows through the Luminous Crown, sending out waves of light that cut through the darkness like a knife. The very ground beneath us shakes as Marina's dark enchantments begin to unravel, their threads coming undone as our light pierces the shadows.

"By the stars that light the sky,
By the earth beneath, where secrets lie,
With fire's warmth and water's flow,
We banish the darkness, let it go.
From ancient roots to cosmic heights,
We reclaim our power, we claim our rights.
No more shadows, no more fear,
In this circle, light draws near.
By our will, by our might,
We end the reign of endless night."

As the final words of our incantation echo through the labyrinth, there is a moment of intense stillness, as if the very world is holding its breath. Then, with a surge of energy, the darkness shatters, dissolving into nothingness. The oppressive weight lifts, and for the first time, the air feels clean, free of the taint of Marina's influence.

We stand in the aftermath, our breaths coming in ragged gasps, but the relief is palpable. The labyrinth, once a twisted maze of dark energy, is now clear, its paths straightened, and its heart purified. Marina's hold over the grove is broken, her power shattered by the strength of our unity and the light of our magick.

Exhausted but triumphant, we make our way back to the grove, where Zephyr waits, his face glowing with pride. The sacred fire burns brighter than ever, its flames a symbol of the victory we've achieved. Together, we've reclaimed our sanctuary, and in doing so, we've forged a bond that will not easily be broken.

As we gather around the fire, the night air filled with the scent of victory and the warmth of camaraderie, I know that this is only the beginning. The path ahead may still be shrouded in mystery, but we will face it together, stronger and more united than ever before. And as the light of the stars guides us, we will continue to unravel the mysteries of our Star seed lineage, discovering the true depths of the ancient magick that flows through our veins. This journey, though fraught with danger, is one that will lead us to a greater understanding of who we are and the power that lies within us all.

CHAPTER 13

DAWN OF THE UNVEILED LIGHT

The night envelops us in its thick, velvety darkness, but the weight of the recent quests is beginning to lift as each group converges back at the heart of the grove. We are weary, our bodies drained from the tasks we've undertaken, yet the air is charged with an electric tension, as if the grove itself is holding its breath in anticipation of the final act. The sacred fire burns brightly at the center, its flames reaching high into the sky, casting long, flickering shadows against the ancient trees surrounding us. These shadows, once a haunting reminder of the darkness that had taken hold of our sanctuary, now herald the dawn of a new beginning.

I stand tall, the Luminous Crown cradled in my hands, its warmth a steady pulse of energy that resonates with the beat of my heart. Its light is a beacon of hope, a symbol of the power we wield as a united coven. "The final stand is upon us," I declare, my voice firm and clear, cutting through the stillness of the grove. "We have purged the labyrinth of Marina's darkness. Now, together, we will cast out the last remnants of her influence from our sacred grove. We will reclaim the light that is our birthright."

Zephyr steps beside me, his presence a calming force amid the tension. His robes shimmer in the firelight, a cascade of silvery fabric that seems to glow with an inner light. His voice is steady, resonant as he begins the Veil-Lifting Chant: "Velum discinditur, veritas revelatur!" (The veil is torn, the truth revealed!). The air around us hums with energy, as if the very fabric of reality is responding to his words. Marina's lingering spells, those remnants of her dark magick that have clung to our sanctuary like a stain, begin to unravel, their power dissipating as the truth is unveiled.

Gideon's voice follows, robust and commanding, as he leads the Final Unraveling Incantation. "Exorior ex umbra, lux perpetua luceat!" (Arise from the shadow, let perpetual light shine!). The Luminous Crown in my hands flares with radiant light, a brilliant burst that floods the grove, illuminating every corner, piercing through the shadows, and seeking out the last vestiges of darkness that Marina had left behind.

The coven, inspired by the fervor of our leaders, unites their voices in a powerful symphony of magick. The grove itself seems to come alive, the ancient trees whispering in forgotten tongues, their energies merging with ours, bolstering our efforts. The light within us, the light of our Star Seed lineage, begins to glow brighter, expanding beyond the confines of our physical forms, connecting us to the stars and the universe itself. This light is not just a source of power; it is a reminder of who we are and where we come from—beings of celestial origin, bearers of ancient wisdom and boundless potential.

Sylvia, her face serene yet resolute, steps forward to deliver the Closing Incantation. Her voice, delicate yet strong, weaves through the air like a thread of silver: "Ultima vincula frangimus, pacem redintegramus!" (We break the final bonds, we restore peace!). Her spell ties together the collective magick, sealing it with a promise of renewal and lasting tranquility. As her words echo through the grove, I feel the last of Marina's darkness dissolve, leaving only light and peace in its wake.

As our chants intertwine, the grove around us begins to transform. The twisted paths straighten, the oppressive mists dissipate, and the scent of fresh blossoms fills the air. It is as if the grove itself is exhaling, releasing the last traces of tension and darkness that have plagued it for so long. Beams of light shower through the canopy, heralding a dawn that symbolizes not just a new day but a rebirth for our coven, a deeper understanding of our shared lineage and the power that flows through our veins.

In this newly sanctified grove, where the fire now blazes with renewed vigor, Gideon and I come together, the trials we've endured forging a bond of deep affection and respect between us. Overwhelmed with relief and joy, Gideon kneels before me, his voice trembling with emotion as he vows his love and devotion. "Soraya," he begins, his voice filled with sincerity and love, "from the moment we met, I knew our paths were meant to intertwine. You are my light in the darkest of times, my strength when I falter, and my inspiration in all things. I vow to stand by your side, to love and support you, to cherish the bond we share, and to honor the light that shines within you. Together, we will create a life guided by love, wisdom, and the strength of our bond."

Tears well in my eyes as I listen to his words, my heart swelling with love for this man who has become my everything.

I take a deep breath, then begin my own vows, my voice steady but filled with emotion. "Gideon, you have shown me a love that is as vast and infinite as the stars. You have been my strength, my protector, and my partner in all things. Today, I vow to love you with all that I am, to stand by your side no matter what lies ahead. I promise to cherish the light we share, to let it guide us through the darkest of times, and to celebrate it in the brightest. Together, we will weave a life of magic and love, bound by the stars and the cosmos that brought us together."

Our shared kiss, under the approving light of the fire and the watchful eyes of our coven, seals our pledge to each other and to the sanctuary we've sworn to protect. The grove erupts in celebration, our triumph over darkness marked by songs of victory and renewal. The air is filled with laughter, the tension of the night replaced with a lightness that lifts our spirits high.

As dawn begins to crest the horizon, its golden light spilling through the trees, we gather for one final moment around the sacred fire. The shadows have been vanquished, Marina's corrupting influence erased. Our grove sings with the magick of freedom and the strength of our united will, a testament to the power we hold as individuals and as a coven.

Zephyr, his role as our guide fulfilled, looks upon us with pride, his eyes reflecting the glow of the rising sun. "The light within us, shared and multiplied, has overcome the deepest shadows," he says, his voice thick with emotion. The coven, moved by his words, shares looks of joy and relief, their spirits lifted by the knowledge that we've emerged victorious, not just in battle but in understanding who we truly are.

Just as we begin to disperse, a rustling at the grove's edge catches my attention. A chill runs down my spine as a shadowy figure emerges from the tree line, its form altered yet unmistakably familiar. The figure pauses, just beyond the reach of the light, its eyes glinting with a malevolent recognition.

"Did you think it was over, Soraya?" the figure hisses, its voice a cold whisper that cuts through the dawn's warmth. "Shadows never die; they only shift. We'll meet again."

As it retreats into the darkness, leaving a trail of eerie silence, my heart pounds—not just with fear, but with an unwavering resolve. This victory, significant though it may be, is just one battle in an ongoing war. With a determined gaze, I turn to my coven, ready to lead them through whatever challenges lie ahead. Our grove remains a place of immense power and deep secrets, ever our sanctuary, ever our battleground.

The dawn continues to rise, its light growing stronger with each passing moment, a symbol of the hope and strength that we carry within us. Together, we stand at the threshold of a new beginning, united and ready to face whatever shadows may come our way. And as we step forward into the light, I know that the journey ahead—into the mysteries of our "Star Seed" lineage, the ancient magick that binds us, and the destiny that awaits— will be one that leads us deeper into the heart of who we are meant to become.

EPILOGUE

THE DUAL WEDDING AND THE UNSEEN ADVERSARY

Six months have passed since we last faced the shadows that threatened our grove, and the passage of time has only strengthened our bonds and deepened our connection to the sacred land we protect. The grove, now brimming with the energy of renewal, seems to pulse with a gentle, steady rhythm as if acknowledging the significance of the day. The sacred fire burns brightly, its flames reflecting the warmth and love that fill the air, mingling with the soft scent of jasmine and lavender that drifts on the evening breeze.

The dual wedding ceremony is the culmination of months of preparation and anticipation, a celebration not only of love but of the triumphs we have shared and the challenges we have overcome. Gideon stands beside me, his gray eyes filled with unwavering devotion and a depth of love that has only grown stronger with time. The firelight dances in his gaze, mirroring the sparks of magick that seem to hum in the air around us.

As I step closer to him, the leaves beneath my feet rustle

softly, whispering secrets of the grove's ancient history. When our hands meet, I feel the familiar, comforting warmth of his touch, grounding me in the reality of this moment despite the surreal beauty that surrounds us.

"You look as radiant as the stars, Soraya," he whispers, his voice carrying a mixture of awe and tenderness.

"And you, my steadfast guardian," I reply, my heart swelling with emotion. "Are you ready to continue weaving our lives together, bound by love and light?"

"Always," he answers, his voice a solemn vow that echoes through the night, as eternal as the stars above us.

High Priestess Malika, her indigo robes shimmering in the firelight, steps forward, holding a braided ribbon that glows softly with the energy of the grove and the light of the stars. The ribbon is a symbol of the cosmic forces that have guided us to this moment. "We gather here, under the watchful eyes of the stars, to celebrate the union of these souls," she begins, her voice resonating with the ancient power that infuses the grove. "With this cord, I bind your hands and hearts, uniting your spirits with the celestial energies that guide us all."

As she wraps the ribbon around our joined hands, I feel a surge of energy, a tangible manifestation of the vows we are about to speak. The ribbon seems to pulse with life, its glow intensifying as it binds us together, a physical representation of the love and commitment we share.

Gideon takes a deep breath, his eyes never leaving mine as he begins to speak his vows. "Soraya, these past six months have only deepened my love for you. You are my light in the darkness, my anchor in the storm, and my partner in all things magical. Today, I vow to continue standing by your side, to support and love you through every challenge and triumph we may face. I promise to honor the light within you, to nurture it and let it guide our way. Together, we will create a life filled with love, wisdom, and the strength of our bond."

Tears well in my eyes as I listen to his words, my heart swelling with love for this man who is my protector, my best friend, and the love of my life. When he finishes, I take a moment to gather myself, then begin my own vows, my voice steady but filled with emotion. "Gideon, you have shown me a love that reaches beyond the stars. You have been my unwavering support, my guardian, and my companion in every journey. Today, I vow to love you with all that I am and to stand by your side no matter what lies ahead. I promise to cherish the light we share, to let it guide us through the darkest of times, and to celebrate it in the brightest. Together, we will weave a life of magick and love, bound by the stars and the cosmos that brought us together."

Malika smiles warmly as she finishes tying the ribbon, sealing our vows with a final knot that pulses with a soft, radiant light. "Bound by fire, earth, and the celestial lights, may your lives together flourish with love, wisdom, and courage," she declares, her voice filled with the weight of ancient blessings.

Beside us, Rowena and Artemis share a look of deep affection, their hands already joined in anticipation of their own vows. As Malika moves to bind their hands with the same braided ribbon, the grove seems to hold its breath once more, the energy in the air thick with expectation.

Rowena speaks first, her voice soft but filled with conviction. "Artemis, these months have shown me that you are my strength, my guide, and my love. With you, I have found peace and a purpose that I never knew was possible. Today, I vow to love you with all that I am, to support you in all that you do, and to cherish the bond we share. Together, we will face whatever challenges come our way, knowing that our love and our magick will see us through."

Artemis squeezes Rowena's hand, her gaze steady and full of love as she responds. "Rowena, you are my heart, my soul, and my partner in all things. With you, I have discovered a love that is as deep and enduring as the earth itself. Today, I vow to stand by your side, to love and support you in all that you do, and to cherish the life we are building together. Together, we will create a world filled with love, light, and the magick that binds us."

As Malika ties the final knot around their hands, the ribbon glows brightly, the energy of their vows merging with the light of the stars and the magick of the grove. "Bound by fire, earth, and the celestial lights, may your lives together flourish with love, wisdom, and courage," she repeats, her voice ringing with the power of the blessings she bestows.

But just as we all bask in the warmth of this sacred moment, a sudden chill sweeps through the grove, cutting through the comfort of the fire. The lanterns flicker wildly, their light casting erratic shadows as the edges of the forest grow darker, more ominous. Malika's eyes narrow, her grip tightening on her staff as she senses the disturbance.

The celebration halts, the joyous atmosphere giving way to a tense silence. From the deepening shadows, a figure emerges—a woman, her presence both haunting and strangely familiar. She moves with an eerie grace, her eyes fixed intently on us, her gaze unwavering as she approaches the fire.

As she steps into the light, every instinct within me flares to life. Malika and I react simultaneously, our hands rising to weave protective spells, the air crackling with our combined power. The intruder stops in her tracks, the intensity of our magick holding her at bay. But as she retreats, something slips from her neck and falls to the leaf-strewn ground—a silver locket, tarnished by time but still glinting with an emblem of ancient power.

I bend to pick it up, my heart racing as I recognize the crest—an emblem linked to a lineage once believed to be lost to history, intimately connected to the original Star Seed guardians. Although its significance eludes me, and I'm uncertain of the full story behind it, the sight of it stirs something deep within me. Malika's gaze locks with mine, her voice low and urgent. "This is no ordinary intruder. She's one of the original guardians, exiled centuries ago. Her return portends something grave."

The fire crackles loudly in the now silent grove, the only sound as the weight of Malika's words sinks in. This woman's emergence from the labyrinth's shadows is no coincidence—it heralds a new threat, perhaps greater than any we have faced before.

Holding the locket, feeling its cold weight in my palm, I sense the pull of a new, daunting chapter about to unfold—a saga that will test our bonds, challenge our magic, and possibly reshape our destinies. The dawn that approaches brings with it the realization of the journey ahead, fraught with unknown dangers but necessary for the survival of our sanctuary.

For within these shadows may lie the keys to our salvation or our undoing.

As I look around at my coven, at the faces of those I love and trust, I know that whatever comes next, we will face it together. The grove, now our sanctuary and our battleground, will witness our continued fight to protect the light within us from the shadows that seek to consume it.

This is not the end, but the beginning of a new chapter—one that will push us to the limits of our power and our resolve. And as we stand here, united under the watchful eyes of the stars, I am ready to lead us into the unknown, confident that our light, the light of the Star Seeds, will guide us through whatever darkness lies ahead.

TO BE CONTINUED